Brett stroked her hair and rubbed slow circles along her back. For the first time in years, Willow felt safe—cared for...

But he was only being nice. When she told him the truth about Sam, there was no telling how he'd act. He might hate her.

"Willow," Brett said softly. "You've got to tell me what's wrong. What happened?"

She sucked in a sharp breath and wiped at her eyes. Brett produced a handkerchief and slipped it into her hands. She wiped her face, then looked up into his.

He had the darkest, most gorgeous green eyes she'd ever seen.

She wanted to soak in his features, but looking at that handsome, strong face only reminded her of her little boy, who looked so much like him that it hurt.

He rubbed her arms with his hands. "Willow, talk to me."

"I...don't know where to begin."

"You said it was a matter of life and death. I noticed the pickup truck outside and the crunched bike. Is that what this is about?"

"I wish it was that simple."

McCULLEN'S SECRET SON

USA TODAY Bestselling Author

RITA HERRON

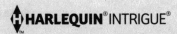

To Aunt Nelda,
for her love of cowboys!
Love, Rita

ISBN-13: 978-0-373-74910-2

McCullen's Secret Son

Copyright © 2015 by Rita B. Herron

PLEASE RECYCLE
THIS PRODUCT IS RECYCLABLE

Recycling programs
for this product may
not exist in your area.

Printed in U.S.A.

HARLEQUIN®
™ www.Harlequin.com

Rita Herron, a *USA TODAY* bestselling author, wrote her first book when she was twelve, but didn't think real people grew up to be writers. Now she writes so she doesn't have to get a real job. A former kindergarten teacher and workshop leader, she traded storytelling to kids for writing romance, and now she writes romantic comedies and romantic suspense. Rita lives in Georgia with her family. She loves to hear from readers, so please write her at PO Box 921225, Norcross, GA 30092-1225, or visit her website, ritaherron.com.

Books by Rita Herron

The Heroes of Horseshoe Creek

Lock, Stock and McCullen
McCullen's Secret Son

Bucking Bronc Lodge

Certified Cowboy
Cowboy in the Extreme
Cowboy to the Max
Cowboy Cop
Native Cowboy
Ultimate Cowboy

Harlequin Intrigue

Cold Case at Camden Crossing
Cold Case at Carlton's Canyon
Cold Case at Cobra Creek
Cold Case in Cherokee Crossing

Visit the Author Profile page at
Harlequin.com for more titles.

CAST OF CHARACTERS

Brett McCullen—The only woman Brett ever loved married another man. But she's in trouble now, and he will put everything on the line to protect her and her son.

Willow James Howard—When her husband is murdered and her son kidnapped, she turns to Brett for help. But will he forgive her when he discovers that her little boy is his son?

Samuel James Howard—Why did someone take him from his mommy?

Leo Howard—Did he love Willow and her little boy, or did he have his own agenda?

Hicks Howard—Does he blame his son Leo for the accident that crippled him?

Gus Garcia—He went to prison for the cattle rustling ring. Was he coerced into making a confession?

Wally Norman & Jasper Day—Leo's partners. Would they kill him and kidnap Sam to get the money Leo stole from them?

Boyle Gates—He's made a fortune with his ranch— but was he in on the cattle rustling scheme?

Doris Benedict—She wanted a family with Leo, but he chose Willow. Did she kill Leo and take Sam because she thinks he's Leo's son?

Eleanor Patterson—She's living in Leo's house— is she lying about knowing Leo?

Gina Tomlin—Willow thought Gina was her friend. Did Gina betray her?

Chapter One

The last place Brett McCullen wanted to be was back in Pistol Whip, especially on the McCullen ranch.

He pulled down the long drive to his family's ranch, Horseshoe Creek, his leg throbbing from his most recent fall. Damn, he loved rodeo and riding.

But maybe at thirty, he was getting too old to bust his butt on the circuit. And last week when he'd woken up in bed with one of the groupies, some hot, busty blonde named Brandy or Fifi— hell, after a while, they all sounded and looked the same—he'd realized that not a soul in the damn world really cared about him.

Or knew the Brett underneath.

Maybe because he was good at the show. Play the part of the bad boy. The fearless rider. The charmer who smiled at the camera and got laid every night.

Easier than getting *real* and chancing getting hurt.

He cut the lights and stared at the farmhouse for a minute, memories suffusing him. He could see him and his brothers, playing horseshoes, practicing roping on the fence posts, riding horses in the pasture, tagging along with their daddy on a cattle drive.

His oldest brother, Maddox, was always the responsible one—and his father's favorite. Ray, two years younger than Brett, was the hellion, the one who landed in trouble, the one who butted heads with their father.

Brett could never live up to his old man's expectations, so he figured why try? Life should be fun. Women, horseback riding, rodeos—it was the stuff dreams were made of.

So he'd left home ten years ago to pursue those dreams and hadn't questioned his decision since.

But Maddox's phone call had thrown him for a loop. How could he deny his father's last request?

Hell, it wasn't like he hadn't loved his old man. He was probably more like him than Maddox or Ray. He'd always thought his father had a wild streak in him, that maybe he'd regretted settling down.

Brett hadn't wanted to make the same mistake.

He walked up the porch steps and reached for the doorknob, then stepped inside, back into a well of family memories that reminded him of all the holidays he'd missed.

Last year, he'd seen daddies shopping with their kids for Christmas trees, and mothers and kids at the park, and couples strolling in the moonlight, and he'd felt alone.

Mama Mary, his dad's housekeeper and cook and the woman who'd taken care of him and his brothers after their mother passed, waddled in and wrapped him into a hug.

"You're a sight for sore eyes," Mama Mary said with a hearty laugh.

Brett buried his head in her big arms, emotions churning through him. He'd forgotten how much he loved Mama Mary, how she could make anything feel all right with a hug and her homemade cooking.

She leaned back to examine him, and patted his flat belly.

"Boy, you've gotten skinny. My biscuits and gravy will fix that."

He laughed. Mama Mary thought she could fix any problem with a big meal. "I've missed you," he said, his voice gruff.

She blinked away tears and ushered him into the kitchen. The room hadn't changed at all—still the checkered curtains and pine table, the plate of sausage and bacon left from breakfast. And as far back as he could remember, she'd always had a cake or pie waiting.

"Sit down now and eat. Then you can see your daddy." She waved him to a chair, and he sank into it. Dread over the upcoming reunion with his father tightened his stomach. Grateful to have a few minutes before he had to confront him, he accepted the peach cobbler and coffee with a smile.

Without warning, the back door opened and his little brother, Ray, stood in the threshold of the door. Ray, with that sullen scowl and cutting eyes. Ray, who always seemed to be mad about something.

Ray gave a clipped nod to acknowledge him, then Mama Mary swept him into a hug, as well. "Oh, my goodness, I can't tell you how much it warms my heart to have you boys back in my kitchen."

Brett gritted his teeth. It wouldn't be for long, though. As soon as he heard what his father had to say, he was back on the road.

A tense silence stretched between them as Mama Mary pushed Ray into a chair and handed him some pie and coffee. Just like they did when they were little, Brett and Ray both obeyed and ate.

"Maddox is on his way home now," Mama Mary said as she refilled their coffee.

Brett and Ray exchanged a furtive look. While the two of them hadn't always seen eye to eye, Ray and Maddox had clashed *big*-time.

Brett had always felt the sting of his big brother's disapproval. According to Maddox, Brett didn't just leave but *ran* at the least hint of trouble.

Footsteps echoed from the front, and Brett braced himself as Maddox stepped into the kitchen, his big shoulders squared, that take-charge attitude wafting off him.

"Now, boys," Mama Mary said before any of them could start tangling. "Your daddy had a rough night. He's anxious to see you, so you'd best get upstairs."

An awkwardness filled the air, but Brett and Ray both stood. His brothers were here for one reason, and none of them liked it.

"I'll go first." Brett mustered up a smile. Pathetic that he'd rather face his father on his deathbed than his brothers.

Ray and Maddox followed, but they waited in the hall as he entered his father's bedroom.

The moment he spotted his father lying in the bed, pale, the veins in his forehead bulging, an oxygen tube in his nose, he nearly fell to his knees with sorrow and regret. He should have at least checked in every now and then.

Although he had come back once five years ago. And he'd hooked up with Willow James. But that night with her had confused the hell out of him, and then he'd fought with Maddox the next day and left again.

"Brett, God, boy, it's good to see you."

Emotions welled in Brett's chest, but he forced himself to walk over to his father's bed.

"Sit down a spell," his father said. "We need to talk."

Brett claimed the wooden chair by the bed, and braced himself for a good dressing-down.

"I want you to know that I'm proud of you, son."

Proud was the last thing he'd expected his father to say.

"But I should have come back more," he blurted.

His father shook his head, what was left of his hair sticking up in white patches. "No, I should have come to some of your rodeos. I kept up with you, though. You're just as talented as I always thought you'd be."

Brett looked in his father's eyes. Joe McCullen looked weak, like he might fade into death any second. But there was no judgment or anger there.

"I'm glad you followed your dreams," his father said in a hoarse voice. "If you'd stayed here and worked the ranch, you'd have felt smothered and hated me for holding you back."

Brett's lungs squeezed for air. His father actually understood him. That was a surprising revelation.

"But there is something you need to take care of while you're here. You remember Willow?"

Brett went very still. How could he have forgotten her? She was his first love, the only woman he'd *ever* loved. But his father had discouraged him from getting too involved with her when he was younger.

So he'd left Pistol Whip, chasing a more exciting lifestyle.

Willow had wasted no time in moving on... and getting married.

She even had a child.

Her last name was what, now? Howard?

"Brett?"

"Yes, I remember her," he said through clenched teeth. "I heard she's married and has a family." That was the real reason he hadn't returned to Pistol Whip more often.

It hurt too damn much to see her with another man.

"That girl's got troubles."

Brett stiffened. "Why are you telling me this?"

"Because I was wrong to encourage you to break up with her," his father murmured. "I've made my mistakes, son. I don't want you to do the same."

His father reached out a shaky hand, and Brett took it, chilled by his cold skin.

"Promise me you'll check on her and her boy," his father murmured.

"That's the reason you wanted to see me?"

"Yes." His father coughed. "Now send Ray in here. I need to talk to him."

Brett squeezed his father's hand, then headed to the door. If his father wanted him to check on Willow, something bad must have happened to her.

His heart hammered at the thought of seeing her again. But he couldn't refuse his father's wishes.

He'd pay her a visit and make sure she was okay. Then he'd get the hell out of Pistol Whip again.

When his father was gone, there was no reason for him to stick around.

Three days later

BRETT MCCULLEN WAS back in town.

Willow James, Willow Howard technically, although she was no longer using her married name, rubbed her chest as if the gesture could actually soothe the ache in her heart. Brett was the only man she'd ever loved. Ever would love.

But he'd walked away from her years ago and never looked back.

She sat in her car at the edge of the graveyard like a voyeur to the family as they said their final goodbyes to their father, Joe. Part of her wanted to go to Brett and comfort him for his loss.

But a seed of bitterness still niggled at her for

the way he'd deserted her. And for the life he'd led since.

He'd always been footloose and fancy-free, a bad-boy charmer who could sweet-talk any girl into doing whatever he wanted.

He'd taken her virginity and her heart with him when he'd left Pistol Whip to chase his dreams of becoming a famous rodeo star.

He'd also chased plenty of other women.

Her heart squeezed with pain again. She'd seen the news footage, the magazine articles and pictures of his awards and conquests.

She'd told herself it didn't matter. She had the best part of him anyway—his son.

Sam.

A little boy Brett knew nothing about.

If Brett saw Sam in town, would he realize the truth? After all, Sam had Brett's deep brown eyes. That cleft in his chin.

The same streak of stubbornness and the love of riding.

A shadow fell across the graveyard, storm clouds gathering, and the crowd began to disperse. She spotted Brett shaking hands with several locals, his brothers doing the same. Then he lifted his head and looked across the graveyard, and for a moment, she thought he was looking straight at her. That he saw her car.

But a second later, Mama Mary loped over and

put her arm around him, and Brett turned back to the people gathered at the service.

Chastising herself for being foolish enough to still care for him after the way he'd hurt her, she started the engine and drove toward her house. She didn't have to worry about Brett. He'd bounce back in the saddle in a day or two and be just fine.

But she had problems of her own.

Not just financial worries, but a no-good husband who she was scared to death of.

Dread filled her as she drove through town and ventured down the side street to the tiny house she'd rented. Her biggest mistake in life was marrying Leo Howard, but she'd been pregnant and on the rebound and had wanted a father for her son.

Leo was no father, though.

Well, at first he'd claimed he was. He'd promised her security and love and a home for her and her little boy.

But as time wore on, she realized Leo had secrets and an agenda of his own.

They hadn't lived together in over three years, but last night he'd come back to town.

Hopefully he had the divorce papers with him, so she could get him out of her life once and for all.

Mentally ticking off her to-do list, she delivered three quilts she'd custom made from orders taken at the antiques store, Vintage Treasures, where she displayed some of her work. When she'd had Sam, she'd known she had to do something to make a living, and sewing was the only skill she had. She'd learned to make clothes, window treatments and quilts from her grandmother, and now she'd turned it into a business.

She did some grocery shopping, then dropped off the rent check. Earlier, she'd left Sam at her neighbor's house, hoping to meet with Leo alone.

She pulled in the drive, noting that Leo had parked his beat-up pickup halfway on the lawn, and that he'd run over Sam's bicycle. Poor Sam. He deserved so much better.

Furious at his carelessness, she threw her Jeep into Park, climbed out and let herself in the house, calling Leo's name as she walked through the kitchen/living room combination, then down the hall to the bedrooms.

When Leo didn't answer, dread filled. He was probably passed out drunk.

Fortified by her resolve to tell him to leave the signed divorce papers so she'd be rid of him for good, she strode to the bedroom. The room was dark, the air reeking of the scent of booze.

Just as she'd feared, Leo was in bed, the covers rumpled, a bottle of bourbon on the bedside table.

Anger churned through her, and she crossed the room, disgusted that he'd passed out in her house. She leaned over to shake him and wake him up, but she felt something sticky and wet on her hand.

She jerked the covers off his face, a scream lodging in her throat. Leo's eyes stared up at her, wide and vacant.

And there was blood.

It was everywhere, soaking his shirt and the sheets…

Leo was dead.

Chapter Two

Willow backed away from the bed in horror. The acrid odor of death swirled around her. There was so much blood…all over Leo's chest. His fingers. Streaking his face where he must have wiped his hand across his cheek.

Nausea rose to her throat, but she swallowed it back, her mind racing.

Leo was…really dead. God…he'd said he was in trouble, but he hadn't mentioned that someone was after him…

She had to get help. Call the police.

Sheriff McCullen.

Her head swam as she fumbled for the phone, but her hand was sticky with blood where she'd touched the bedding.

She trembled, ran into the bathroom and turned on the water, desperate to cleanse herself of the ugly smell. She scrubbed her hand with soap, reality returning through the fog of shock.

Where was the killer? Was he still in the house?

She froze, straining as she listened for signs of an intruder, but the house seemed eerily silent.

Sam… Lord help me. Her neighbor would probably drop Sam off any minute. She couldn't let him come home to this.

Panicked, she dried her hands, then ran for the phone again. But a shadow moved across the room, and she suddenly realized she wasn't alone.

Terrified, she dived for the phone, but the figure lunged at her and grabbed her from behind. Willow screamed and tried to run, but he wrapped big beefy hands around her and immobilized her.

His rough beard scraped her jaw as he leaned close to her ear. "You aren't going to call the cops."

Fear shot through her. "No, no police."

He tightened his grip around her, choking the air from her lungs. "If you do, you'll end up like your husband."

Willow shook her head. "Let me go and I promise I'll do whatever you say."

A nasty chuckle rumbled in her ear. "Oh, you'll do what we want, Willow. That is, if you want to see your little boy again."

"What?" Willow gasped.

He twisted her head back painfully, as if he was going to snap her neck. She tried to breathe, but the air was trapped in her lungs. "Please… don't hurt him."

"That's up to you." He shoved her head forward, and she felt the barrel of his gun at the back of her head. "We'll be in touch with instructions."

Then he slammed the butt of the gun against her head. Pain shot through her skull, and the world spun, the room growing dark as she collapsed.

BRETT HAD MUDDLED his way through the funeral and tacked on his polite semicelebrity smile as the neighbors offered condolences and shared the casseroles that had been dropped off.

He didn't know why people ate when they were grieving, but Mama Mary kept forcing food and tea in his hands, and he didn't have the energy to argue. He'd grown accustomed to cameras, to putting on a happy face when his body was screaming in pain from an injury he'd sustained from a bull ride.

He could certainly do it today.

"Thank you for coming," he said as he shook another hand.

Betty Bane's daughter Mandy slipped up beside him and gave him a flirtatious smile. She looked as if she'd just graduated high school. *Jailbait.* "Hey, Brett, I'm so sorry about your daddy."

"Thanks." He started to step away, but she raised her cell phone. "I know it may not be a good time, but can I get a selfie with you? My friends won't believe I actually touched *the* Brett McCullen!"

She giggled and plastered her face so close to his that her cheek brushed his. "Smile, Brett!"

Unbelievable. She wanted him to pose. To pretend he hadn't just buried his old man.

He bit the inside of his cheek to keep from telling her she was shallow and insensitive, then extricated himself as soon as she got the shot. He shoved his plate on the counter, wove through the crowd and stepped outside, then strode toward the stable.

He wanted to be alone. Needed a horse beneath him, the fresh air blowing in his face and the wild rugged land of Horseshoe Creek to make him forget about the man he and his brothers had just put six feet under.

Or…he could take a trip down to The Silver Bullet, the honky-tonk in town, and drown his sorrow in booze and a woman.

But the thought of any female other than the one he'd left behind in Pistol Whip didn't appeal to him. Besides, if the press got wind he was there, they'd plaster his picture all over the place. And he didn't need that right now. Didn't want them following him to the ranch or intruding on his brothers.

A heaviness weighed in his chest, and he saddled up a black gelding, climbed atop and sent the horse into a sprint. Storm clouds had rolled in earlier, casting a grayness to the sky and adding to the bleakness of the day.

He missed the stars, but a sliver of moonlight wove between the clouds and streaked the land with golden rays, just enough to remind him how beautiful and peaceful the rugged land was.

To the west lay the mountains, and he pictured the wild mustangs running free. He could practically hear the sound of their hoofs beating the ground as the horses galloped over the terrain.

Cattle grazed in the pastures, and the creek gurgled nearby, bringing back memories of working a cattle drive when he was young, of campfires with his father and brothers, of fishing in Horseshoe Creek.

He'd also taken Willow for rides across this land. They'd had a picnic by the creek and skinny-dipped one night and then…made love.

It was the sweetest moment he'd ever had with a woman. Willow had been young and shy and innocent, but so damn beautiful that, even as the voice in his head cautioned him not to take her, he'd stripped her clothes anyway.

They'd made love like wild animals, needy and hungry, as if they might never be touched like that again.

But he and his brothers had been fighting for months. His father had started drinking and carousing the bars, restless, too. He'd met him at the door one night when he'd been in the barn with Willow, and warned Brett that if he ever wanted to follow his dreams, he needed to leave Willow alone.

His father's heart-to-heart, a rarity for the two of them, had lit a fire inside him and he'd had to scratch that wandering itch. Like his father said, if he didn't pursue rodeo, he'd always wonder if he'd missed out.

That was ten years ago—the first time he'd left. He'd only been back once since, five years ago. Then he'd seen Willow again...

He climbed off the horse, tied him to a tree by the creek, then walked down to the bank, sat down, picked up a stone and skipped it across the water. The sound of the creek gurgling mingled sweetly with the sound of Willow's voice calling his name in the moonlight when they'd made love right here under the stars.

He'd made it in the rodeo circuit now. He had fame and belt buckles and more women than any man had a right to have had.

But as he mourned his father, he realized that in leaving, he'd missed something, too.

Willow. A life with her. A real home. A family.

Someone who'd love him no matter what. Whether he lost an event, or got injured and was too sore to ride, or...too old.

He buried his head in his hands, sorrow for his

father mingling with the fact that coming back here only made him want to see Willow again.

But she was married and had a kid.

And even if she had troubles like his father said, she could take care of them herself. She and that husband of hers…

He didn't belong in her life anymore.

WILLOW ROUSED FROM unconsciousness, the world tilting as she lifted her head from the floor. For a moment, confusion clouded her brain, and she wondered what had happened.

But the stench of death swirled through the air, and reality surfaced, sending a shot of pure panic through her.

Leo was dead. And a man had been in the house, had attacked her.

Had said Sam was gone…

She choked on a scream, and was so dizzy for a second, she had to hold her head with her hands to keep from passing out. Nausea bubbled in her throat, but she swallowed it back, determined not to get sick.

She had to find her son.

A sliver of moonlight seeped through the curtains, the only light in the room. But it was enough for her to see Leo's body still planted in her bed, his blood soaking his clothes and the sheets like a red river.

Who was the man in the house? Was he still here? And why would he kidnap Sam?

Shaking all over, she clutched the edge of the dresser and pulled herself up to stand. Her breathing rattled in the quiet, but she angled her head to search the room. It appeared to be empty. She staggered to the kitchen and living room.

Both were empty.

Nerves nearly immobilized her, but she held on to the wall and made herself go to Sam's room. Tears blurred her eyes, but she swiped at them, visually scanning the room and praying that the man had lied. That her little four-year-old boy was inside, safe and sound. That this was all some kind of sick, twisted dream.

Except the blood on the bed and Leo's body was very real.

At first glance, her son's room seemed untouched. His soccer ball lay on the floor by the bed, his toy cars and trucks in a pile near the block set. His bed was still made from this morning, his superhero pillow on top, next to the cowboy hat he'd begged for on his birthday.

But this morning his horse figurines had been arranged by the toy barn and stable where he'd set them up last night when he was playing rodeo. She was afraid he had his father's blood in him.

The horses were knocked over now, the toy barn broken. Sam was supposed to be at Gina's...

Her mind racing, she hurried to retrieve her

cell phone from her purse and called her neighbor. *Please let Sam still be there.*

The phone rang three times, then Gina finally answered. "Hello."

"Gina, it's Willow. Is Sam there?"

"No, his father picked him up. I hope that was all right."

Willow pressed her hand to her mouth to stifle a sob. So Sam had come home with Leo.

Which meant he'd probably witnessed Leo's murder.

Fear squeezed the air from her lungs. The man who'd attacked her, warned her not to call the police, that she'd hear from him…

But when?

And what was happening to Sam now?

BRETT FELT WRENCHED from the inside out. He'd been living on adrenaline, the high of being a star, of having women throwing themselves at him, and everyone wanting a piece of him for so long, that he didn't know what to do with himself tonight.

He knew one thing, though—he did not want a picture of himself at his father's graveside all over the papers. He'd told his publicist that, and banned her from making any public announcement about his father's death.

Grieving for his father and returning to his

hometown were private, and he wanted to keep it that way.

Night had fallen, the cows mooing and horses roaming the pastures soothing as he rose from the creek embankment, climbed on his horse and headed back to the farmhouse. The ranch hands would have been fed by now, the days' work done, until sunrise when the backbreaking work started all over again.

If he had to stay here a couple of days to wait on the reading of the will, maybe he'd get up with the hands and pitch in. Nothing like working up a sweat hauling hay, rounding cattle or mending fences to take his mind off the fact that he'd never see his daddy again.

It made him think about his mother and how he'd felt at eight when she'd died. He'd run home from the school bus that day, anxious for a hug and to tell her about the school rodeo he'd signed up for, but the minute he'd walked in and seen his daddy crying, he'd known something was terribly wrong.

And that his life would never be the same.

Damn drunk driver had turned his world upside down.

Shaking off the desolate feeling the memory triggered, he reminded himself that he had made a success out of himself. He had friends...well, not friends, really. But he was surrounded by people all the time.

He'd thought that the crowd loving him would somehow fill the empty hole inside him. That having folks cheer for him and yell his name meant they loved him.

But they loved the rodeo star. If he didn't have that, no one would give him a second look.

The breeze invigorated him as he galloped across the pasture. When he reached the ranch, he spotted Maddox outside with a woman. Moonlight played off the front yard, and he yanked on the reins to slow his horse as he realized he was intruding on a private moment. He steered the animal behind a cluster of trees, waiting in the shadows.

Maddox was on his knees, and so was the woman he was with. They were kissing like they couldn't get enough of each other.

The two of them finally pulled back for a breath, and Brett froze as he saw Maddox slide a ring on the woman's finger.

His brother had just proposed.

He should be glad for Maddox. His older brother had taken his mother's death hard, and he and their daddy had been close.

Maddox had obviously found love. Good for him.

He tightened his fingers around the reins, turned the gelding around and rode back to the stables.

Something about seeing Maddox with that woman made him feel even more alone than he had before.

WILLOW COULDN'T STAND to look at Leo's dead body.

She needed to call the police. But what if the killer was watching her and the sheriff came, and he saw her and hurt her son?

She paced to the living room, frantic. She needed help. She couldn't do this alone.

But calling Sheriff McCullen was out of the question.

Brett's face flashed behind her eyes. She hadn't talked to him since he'd left five years ago. When they'd made love that night, she'd thought that Brett might be rethinking his career, that he might have missed her. That he might have contemplated returning to her.

But the next day he'd left town without a word.

Still, he was Sam's father. Even if he didn't know it.

Heaven help her…he'd be furious with her for not telling him. Although years ago, he'd made it plain and clear that he didn't intend to settle down or stay in Pistol Whip. A wife and a child would have cramped his style and kept him from chasing his dreams.

And Willow refused to trap him. He would only have resented her and Sam.

Would he help her now?

She picked up Sam's photo and studied her precious little boy's face, and she decided it didn't matter. It might be a bad time for Brett, but her son was in danger, and she'd do anything to save him.

Her hand trembled as she phoned the McCullen house. Mama Mary answered, and she asked to speak to Brett.

"He's out riding, can I take a message or tell him who called?"

"It's Willow James. And it's important," she said. "Can you give me his cell phone number?"

"Why sure thing, Ms. Willow." Mama Mary repeated it and Willow ended the call abruptly, then called Brett's mobile. Nerves gripped her as she waited on him to answer. What if he didn't pick up? He might not want to talk to her at all.

The phone clicked, then his deep voice echoed back. "Hello."

"Brett, it's Willow."

Dead silence, then his sharp intake of breath. "Yeah?"

"I'm sorry about your father," she said quickly. "But I…need to see you tonight."

"What?" His voice sounded gruff, a note of surprise roughening it.

"Please," Willow cried. "I…can't explain, but it's a matter of life and death."

Chapter Three

Brett clenched his phone in a white-knuckled grip as he paced the barn. He hadn't seen or talked to Willow in years, and she hadn't attended his father's funeral today. Even as he'd told himself he didn't care if she came, he'd looked for her.

But now she wanted to see him?

It's a matter of life and death.

What the hell was going on?

He cleared his throat. Once upon a time, he'd have jumped and run at a moment's notice if Willow had called. But she was a married woman now. "What's wrong, Willow?"

"I can't explain on the phone," she said, her voice strained. "Please, Brett...I don't know what else to do. Who to call."

His gut tightened at the desperation in her voice. "Willow—"

"Please, I'm begging you. I need your help."

"All right, I'll be right there." He didn't bother to ask for her address. He knew where she lived.

Mama Mary had managed to drop it in the conversation once when he'd had a weak moment and had called home.

He'd already unsaddled his horse, so he jogged back to the house and climbed in his pickup truck.

Thankfully, Maddox and his lady friend had gone inside, and he had no idea where Ray was, so he didn't have to explain to anyone. Not that he had to tell them where he was going.

He hadn't answered to anyone in a long time.

Well, except for his publicist and fans and the damn press.

He drove from the ranch, winding down the drive to the road leading into town, the quiet of the wilderness a reprieve from the cities he'd traveled to. A few miles, and he drove through the small town, noting that not much had changed.

At this late hour, the park was empty, the general store closed, yet country music blared from The Silver Bullet, and several vehicles were parked in the lot. He wasn't surprised to see Ray's. He was probably drowning his sorrows.

Inside, the booze and music was always flowing, the women footloose and fancy-free. Just his type.

Another night maybe…

He turned down the street toward Willow's, anxiety needling him. He'd never stopped loving her. Wanting her.

But she was taken. And he had a different life

now. A life he'd chosen. Another rodeo coming up, another town…

Children's bikes and toys dotted the yards, suggesting the neighborhood catered to young families. The house at the end of her block, a small rustic log cabin, was Willow's and was set way back from the road, offering privacy. A beat-up pickup truck that had obviously run over the child's bike sat crooked, half in the drive, half in the yard.

His father had said Willow had troubles… Did it have to do with the man she'd married? Judging from the sloppy way the truck was parked, and the fact that he'd run over the bike, maybe he'd been drinking…

Not your problem, Brett.

Except that Willow said she needed him.

He scanned the outside to see if her old man was lurking around. Did he know that Brett and his wife had had a romantic relationship years ago?

He braced himself for trouble as he parked and walked up to the front door. Barring a low-burning light in the bedroom, the house looked dark.

The hair on the back of his neck prickled as he rang the doorbell. Something didn't feel right…

He waited several seconds, then knocked and called through the door, "Willow, it's me. Brett."

The sound of footsteps on the other side

echoed, then the lock turned, and the door squeaked open. His breath stalled in his chest as Willow appeared, the door cracking just enough to see her face.

"Brett?" Her face looked ashen, and a streak of blood darkened her hair.

"Yeah, it's me."

Panicked at the sight of her disheveled state, he pushed open the door and stepped inside. "What the hell's wrong?"

She slammed the door shut, then locked it and turned to face him, her eyes wide with fear. "Help me," she whispered as she threw herself into his arms.

Brett's stomach churned as he pulled her trembling body against him and wrapped his arms around her.

WILLOW SANK INTO Brett's arms, the terror she'd felt since she'd arrived home pouring out of her as he held her. She tried to battle the tears, but they overflowed, soaking his shirt.

"Shh, it's all right," Brett murmured into her hair. "Whatever's wrong, we can fix it."

She shook her head against him. "That's just it, I don't know if I can."

Brett stroked her hair, and rubbed slow circles along her back. For the first time in years, she felt safe. Cared for.

But he was only being nice. He had his own life,

and when she confessed the truth about Sam, there was no telling how he'd react. He might hate her.

Or he might leave town and not get involved in her troubles. A murder case could ruin his reputation.

But really—none of that mattered. Not when Sam was in danger.

"Willow," Brett said softly. "Honey, you've got to tell me what's wrong. What happened?"

Brett slipped a handkerchief into her hands and she wiped her face. Then she looked up into his eyes.

He had the darkest, most gorgeous eyes she'd ever seen. Eyes she'd gotten lost in years ago.

She wanted to soak in his features, but looking at that handsome, strong face only reminded her of her little boy who looked so much like him that it hurt.

He rubbed her arms. "Willow, talk to me."

"I...don't know where to begin." *With the body of her dead husband? Or Sam?*

"You said it was a matter of life and death. I know you're married, that you have a little boy." She squeezed her eyes shut, unable to look at him for a moment.

"I noticed the pickup truck outside and the crunched bike. Is that what this is about?"

"I wish it was that simple," she said on a shaky breath.

Brett led her over to the sofa and she sank onto

it, her legs giving way. He joined her, but this time he didn't touch her.

"Your husband? Is he here? Did he hurt you?"

Emotions threatened to overcome her again, and she glanced at the phone, willing it to ring. Willing the caller to tell her how to get her little boy back and end this horror.

"Did he?" Brett asked, his voice harsh with anger.

She shook her head. "Not exactly."

Brett shot up from the seat, his jaw twitching. "Come on, Willow, tell me what the hell is going on."

"He's dead," Willow blurted. "Leo is…dead."

Brett went stone still and stared at her. "What do you mean, *dead*?"

"In there," Willow said. "When I got home tonight, I found him."

He glanced around the bedroom, then exhaled noisily. "How did he die?"

"Someone shot him." Her voice cracked. "There's blood…everywhere."

Brett released a curse and strode to the bedroom. Willow jumped up and raced after him, trembling as he flipped on the overhead light. The stark light lit the room, accentuating the grisly scene in her bed. Leo staring at the ceiling with dead eyes. Blood on his clothes and the sheets.

Brett choked back an obscenity. "Who shot him?"

"I don't know," Willow whispered. "I...found him and was going to call the police, but then a man jumped me."

Brett pivoted, his eyes searching her face, mouth pinched with anger as he lifted his hand and touched her forehead. She didn't realize she'd been bleeding, but he drew his hand back and she saw blood streaking his finger. "He hurt you?"

"I'm all right. He grabbed me from behind, and he said... He told me not to call the police, that he...had Sam."

"Sam?"

Willow's lungs strained for air. "My little boy. He has him, Brett. And he said if I called the police, I'd never see him again."

BRETT GRITTED HIS TEETH. "You mean he kidnapped your child?"

"Yes," Willow cried. "I have to get him back."

Brett stared at the man lying dead in Willow's bed.

Her husband.

He'd never met the man but had heard he was a businessman, that he'd done well for himself.

So why had someone wanted him dead? And why kidnap Willow's son?

"I don't know what to do," Willow said "I... can't leave Leo there. But if I call the sheriff, he'll send police and crime workers, and I might never see Sam again."

Cold fury seized Brett's insides. What kind of person threatened a small child?

"How old is Sam?" he asked.

"Four," Willow said. "He's just a little guy, Brett. He has to be terrified." Her voice cracked again, her terror wrenching Brett's heart. "And if he saw Leo murdered, then he may be traumatized."

He also might be able to identify the killer.

But Brett bit back that observation because it would only frighten Willow more.

If her son could identify her husband's shooter, the killer might not let Sam live anyway, no matter what Willow did.

Brett tried to strip the worry from his voice. "What does this man want from you, Willow?"

"I have no idea." She looked up at him with swollen, tear-stained eyes. "He said to wait for a call."

Brett turned away from the sight of the bloody, dead man. "I know you're scared, but think about it—why would this man take Sam? Did your husband have a lot of money?"

Willow shook her head back and forth, sending her hair swaying. It was tangled from where she'd run her hands through it, the long strands even more vibrant with streaks of gold and red than he remembered.

He tried to dismiss memories of running his hands through it, of the way it felt tickling his belly when she'd loved him, but an image teased his mind anyway.

"Are you sure? Maybe he had some investments? Stocks?"

"If he had any money, I didn't know about it," Willow said. "He didn't even have a savings or checking account in town. It's one of the things we argued about."

Brett arched a brow. He didn't have a bank account in town—which meant he was probably hiding one somewhere else? "One of the things?"

Her face paled. "Yes." She closed her eyes, a pained sound escaping her. "You might as well know. We weren't getting along. We hadn't for a while. Leo moved out three years ago."

Brett tried to assimilate that information. "What has he been doing?"

"I don't know," she said in a choked whisper.

"Was he giving you any money to live on? Helping out with the boy?"

Willow worried her bottom lip with her teeth. "No. He...didn't want to be a father to Sam."

An odd note crept into her voice.

"What kind of father doesn't want to be there for his kid?"

Willow didn't respond, making Brett even more curious about her husband and how he'd treated her.

"Willow, talk to me. What happened between you two? Was he abusing you and Sam?"

Willow cut her eyes away. "When we met, he was kind, charming. But the last year he'd been drinking too much, and his temper erupted."

"And he took it out on you and Sam?"

Willow shrugged. "At first it was just verbal. But…he hit me once. Then he started in on Sam, and I told him to leave." A fierce protectiveness strengthened her voice. "I would never let him hurt my son. I asked him for a divorce."

"How did he take that?"

"He was angry, but he left. Frankly…I think he wanted out."

"You don't know what he's been doing since?"

"No, I have no idea."

He was obviously in trouble.

Dammit. Even though he and his brother were hardly talking, Brett's first instinct was to call Maddox.

But that would endanger Willow's son.

Besides, Maddox had always been by the book. He'd want to call in the authorities, issue an Amber Alert, all the things they should be doing.

But if they did those things, Willow's little boy could end up dead like his father.

He couldn't allow that to happen.

So he made a snap decision. He'd bury Leo's body and protect Willow until they found Sam.

Chapter Four

Willow couldn't drag her eyes away from Leo's dead body. She couldn't believe this was happening.

She'd hated that her marriage had fallen apart, but it hadn't been right from the beginning. She'd never loved Leo and he knew it.

And truthfully, she didn't think he'd ever loved her.

But she'd been hurt with Brett, and lonely and a single pregnant woman with nowhere to turn. Leo had offered her security and comfort.

For a little while. Then everything had changed and the charming man who'd swept in like a hero had disappeared and become…someone she was afraid of.

Someone Sam was afraid of.

That was when she'd known she had to get out.

The blood on her hands mocked her. She hadn't loved Leo but she'd never wished him dead.

And where was her precious little boy? Was he safe? Hurt? Scared?

A tremor rippled through her. Of course he was scared. He'd been taken from his home.

"We'll bury him on the ranch somewhere," Brett said. "It's too dangerous to do it in your neighborhood."

Willow rubbed her hands up and down her arms as if to warm herself. "But what about Maddox? He's the sheriff and…your brother."

Brett's look darkened. "I know that," Brett said. "I'll talk to him and explain once we get your little boy back."

Willow's heart constricted. "I'm sorry for putting you in this position, Brett. You could get in trouble with the law. But…I didn't know who else to call."

Brett clasped her arms and forced her to look at him. "Don't worry about me, Willow. I can handle whatever happens. But we can't go to Maddox yet. We have to play by this bastard's rules, until we find Sam."

How could she argue with that? She'd give her life for her son's.

And if Brett knew that Sam was his, he'd do the same.

He probably would anyway, just because he was a McCullen. Joe McCullen had taught his boys old-fashioned values, that men were supposed to protect women and children.

Brett moved over by the bed. "I need to get him in the back of my pickup."

"Why? Aren't we going to bury him in the backyard?"

"No," Brett said. "You live in a neighborhood. And if anyone comes asking about Leo and is suspicious, this is the first place they'd look." He glanced down at the floor and indicated the braided rug. "Let's wrap him in the sheet and I can use the rug to slide him outside."

"But what if a neighbor sees us?"

Brett's jaw tightened. "Your house is set far enough back from the road, so unless someone is in the drive, we should be all right. But I'll move my truck up to the garage and we can go through there just to be safe."

Willow agreed, although she knew what they were doing was wrong. *Illegal*. That they could both be charged.

But nothing mattered now except saving Sam.

BRETT HATED THE FEAR in Willow's eyes. If he had hold of the bastard who had hurt her and taken her little boy, he'd pound his head in.

He started to roll Leo in the sheet, but doubts hit him. He'd seen enough crime shows to know that as soon as he touched the man or the bedding, he was contaminating evidence. Evidence that could lead to the killer and the person who had abducted Sam.

Besides, he'd gotten in a sticky situation once. Had been accosted by the jealous lover of a rodeo groupie he'd dated, a man who'd tried to make it look as if he was the guilty party. He'd seen how the police handled the situation. If it hadn't been for a savvy detective who paid attention to detail, Brett might have gone to jail.

Maybe he *should* call Maddox.

But the kidnapper's warning taunted him. Willow's little boy was in danger.

He couldn't take the chance on that child getting hurt. Pain tugged at his chest. He'd once thought he and Willow would have a family together.

But he'd left and she'd met Leo, and their lives had gone down another path.

Still, her little boy shouldn't suffer.

He removed his phone and snapped some pictures of the man, the wounds to his chest, the blood on the sheets, and the room.

"What are you doing?" Willow asked.

"We'll be destroying evidence here," Brett said. "I should document how we found Leo to show Maddox when we tell him."

Willow's face paled. "I can't believe this is happening, Brett. I…don't know why anyone would want to kill Leo."

Brett clenched his jaw. "We'll talk about that once we take care of him." He studied the scene again, then snapped a picture of the bullet hole in Leo's chest. "Do you have plastic gloves?"

She nodded and hurried to the kitchen. Seconds later, she returned with two pairs of latex gloves and they both pulled them on. "Let's roll him in the sheet onto the floor. Then I'll wrap him in the rug and drag him outside."

Tears glittered in Willow's eyes, but she jumped into motion to help him. The man's shirt was soaked in blood, his eyes wide with shock, his mouth slack, one hand curled into a fist as if he might have been holding something.

If he had, the killer had taken it.

"Did Leo own a gun?"

"What man in Wyoming doesn't?" Willow asked.

"What kind?"

"A pistol and a shotgun," Willow said. "But he took them when he moved out."

"Look around for bullet casings. Maddox will want them to help with the case." Willow walked around, searching the floor and the bathroom, but shook her head. "I don't see any."

"How about you? Do you have a gun?"

Willow shook her head. "No, I didn't want weapons in the house with Sam."

Good point.

"When did you learn about crime scenes?" Willow asked.

Brett shrugged. He didn't intend to share the

story about that debacle with the rodeo groupie. "Television."

She frowned as if that surprised her, but he wrapped the sheet around Leo, gritting his teeth as Willow's husband stared up at him in death.

Blood had dried onto the sheet and soaked through to the mattress. Rigor had set in and Leo was a deadweight. Willow gasped as he eased the man to the rug.

"Strip the rest of the bedding," Brett said. "And bag it. We'll keep it to give to Maddox later."

Willow looked ill, but she rushed back to the kitchen and returned a moment later with a big garbage bag.

While he wrapped the top sheet tighter around Leo, she stripped the fitted sheet and comforter and jammed it in the plastic bag. Her ragged breathing rasped between them as she added the pillowcases, then she stood and stared at the bed for a moment as if she'd never be able to sleep in it again.

Brett wanted to comfort her, but he needed to get rid of Leo's corpse before anyone discovered what they'd done.

THE SCENT OF the blood on her sheets and the image of Leo lying dead in her bed made Willow feel ill.

She didn't know how she'd ever sleep in this room again.

"What should I do with these?"

"We'll bury them with Leo."

The thought of digging a hole for her husband sent bile to her throat. But as Brett dragged Leo's body on that rug into the hall, she glanced in Sam's room again, and determination rifled through her.

That empty room nearly brought her to her knees.

Determined to bring her son home no matter what, she followed Brett with the garbage bag. He pulled Leo through the hallway to the kitchen. She opened the garage door, and he left Leo in the garage, then backed his pickup around to the exterior garage door, which faced the side of the drive.

Anger at Leo mushroomed inside her.

Leo had a temper, was manipulative and secretive and…he had gotten rough with her more than once. But the day he'd put his hand on Sam, she'd ordered him to leave and told him she wanted a divorce.

Nobody would hurt her baby.

Except Sam might be hurt now… All because of the man she'd exchanged vows with. She leaned over Leo and stared at him, a mother's temper boiling over. "What did you do to get my son kidnapped?"

Of course he didn't answer. He simply laid there with his mouth slack and his eyes bulging.

If possible, his face looked even paler beneath the kitchen lights.

Brett appeared a second later, wiping sweat from his brow with the back of his sleeve. He planted his hands on his hips and looked down at Leo, then up at her.

"Are you okay, Willow?"

A sob caught in her throat, and she shook her head. "How can I be all right when Sam is missing? When he might be crying for me right now?"

Silence stretched full of tension for a minute. "Then let's get this done."

Brett sounded resigned, and Willow questioned again whether she should have called him. But what else could she do?

Brett knelt and grabbed the end of the rug, and Willow decided she couldn't allow him to do this alone. She set the garbage bag down, flipped off the garage light so they couldn't be seen through the front window, then grabbed the opposite side of the rug and helped Brett drag Leo through the garage.

She was heaving for breath by the time they reached the threshold of the exterior door. Leo's body was so heavy that she didn't know how Brett would lift him.

The garage door was situated on the side of the house and wasn't visible from the street, but in silent agreement they paused to check and make sure there weren't any cars passing or anyone walking by.

"It's clear." Brett stooped down, scooped Leo up—still wrapped in the rug—and threw him over his shoulder. She bit down on her lip to stifle a gasp as Leo's arm swung over Brett's back. The dried blood on his hand and face looked macabre in the moonlight.

Brett struggled for a minute with the weight, then maneuvered Leo's body into the truck bed. He climbed in and threw an old blanket over the body, and she tossed the bag of linens in the back with him.

"I'd tell you to stay here," Brett said, "but it's not safe, Willow. Come with me and I'll bring you back later."

The last thing Willow wanted to do tonight was bury Leo, but she had started this and she had to see it through. At least until she got Sam back.

"Let me get my phone in case the kidnapper calls tonight."

BRETT SAID A SILENT prayer that the kidnapper would call, but as Willow went to retrieve her phone and purse, he had a bad feeling. What did the kidnapper want?

Money? Or something else?

All questions to pursue once they got rid of Leo's body.

Damn, he couldn't believe he was doing this.

Actively covering up a crime. If his agent and his fans found out, his career would be over.

Hell, if Maddox didn't help him out when he finally explained things, his life as a free man would be over.

But he couldn't let Willow down.

His phone buzzed, and he checked the caller ID. Kitty. Another pesky immature groupie.

Dammit, he'd slept with her twice, then broken it off, but she'd become obsessed with him. He'd warned her that he'd take out a restraining order if she didn't leave him alone.

He'd hoped coming home for a while might give her the time and distance she needed to move on.

Willow locked the house and closed the garage door and he let the call roll to voice mail, then covered Leo's body in the bed of the truck. If he got stopped…no, that was not going to happen.

He removed the latex gloves and Willow did the same. He stuffed both pairs in his pocket, then opened the passenger side for Willow, and she climbed onto the seat, her hand shaking as she gripped the seat edge. The wind kicked up, stirring leaves and rattling the windows as he hurried to the driver's side, jumped in and started the engine.

The moon disappeared behind storm clouds as he eased onto the street. Senses on alert, Brett searched right and left, then in the rearview mirror, looking for someone who might be watching.

For all he knew, the killer/kidnapper might have hung around to see if Willow called the law.

Willow leaned against the doorframe, looking lost and shaken, and so terrified that Brett's heart broke. In spite of the fact that he was digging a hole for himself with the law and his own brother, he pulled her hand in his.

"We'll get Sam back, Willow. I promise."

"But what if—"

"Shh." He brought her hand to his mouth and kissed her fingers. "Everything will be all right. I swear."

Tears trickled down her cheeks, and she broke into another sob. Brett pulled her over beside him and wrapped his arm around her as he drove. She collapsed against him, her head against his chest, her arm slipped around his waist.

The two of them had ridden just this way in high school, hugging and kissing as they'd driven up to Make-Out Point. But tonight, they wouldn't be making out or…making love.

Tonight they were hiding her husband's body, and she was almost despondent over her missing son.

Still checking over his shoulder as he turned onto the highway, a siren wailed from the right, and he tensed. A fire engine, ambulance, police?

Suddenly blue lights swirled against the night sky as a police car careened around the corner and flew toward them.

Brett's chest constricted. He was about to get caught with a dead body in his truck.

SAM CURLED INTO a little ball, hugged his knees to his chest and leaned against the wall. He was shaking so badly, he thought he might pee his pants. He hadn't done that since he was two.

Where was he? And why had that man with the bandana over his face grabbed him and thrown him in the trunk of his car?

Sam hated that trunk. He hated the dark.

Swiping at tears, he clutched the ratty teddy bear the man had tossed into the room with him. He didn't want the old dusty thing. He wanted his dinosaur and his mommy and his room with all his toys.

But he clutched the bear anyway because it made him feel like he wasn't all alone.

Outside the dark room, footsteps pounded and two men's voices sounded. Loud. Mad. They were barking at each other like dogs.

They had been mad at Daddy. Then one of them had pulled that gun and shot him.

Sam closed his eyes, trying to forget the red blood that had flown across the bed like a paintball exploding. Except it wasn't paint.

He couldn't forget it.

Or that choked gurgling sound Daddy had made.

He started shaking and had to hug his legs with his arms to keep his knees from knocking. He had to be quiet. Make them think he was asleep or they'd come back and get him.

Daddy was dead.

And if he didn't do what they told him, he'd be dead, too.

Chapter Five

Willow clenched her clammy hands together as the sirens wailed closer. Dear Lord, had someone seen them leave with Leo's body?

Brett laid a hand over hers. "It'll be all right."

But they both knew it wouldn't be all right. They'd lose precious time explaining themselves to the police, and even then, they would go to jail and the kidnapper might hurt Sam.

Brett slowed and pulled off the road, but they were both shocked when the police car raced on by.

His relieved breath punctuated the air. "Whew, I thought they had us."

"Me, too." She wiped at the perspiration trickling down the side of her face, but she was trembling so badly a pained sound rumbled from her throat.

Brett pulled her to him for a moment and soothed her. "Hang in there, Willow. I'm here."

She nodded, those words giving her more comfort than he could imagine. She didn't think she could hold it together tonight if she was alone.

They sat there for several seconds, but finally Brett pulled away and inched back onto the road. By the time they reached the ranch, her breathing had finally steadied.

She had always loved Horseshoe Creek, but tonight she found no peace in the barren stretch of land where Brett parked.

Brett kept looking in the rearview mirror and across the property as if he thought they might have been followed. The land seemed eerily quiet, the wind whistling off the ridges, whipping twigs and tumbleweed across the dirt as if a windstorm was brewing.

This rocky area was miles away from the big farmhouse where Brett had grown up, the pasture where the McCullen cattle grazed, from the stables housing their working horses and the bungalows where the ranch hands lived.

The truck rumbled to a stop, and Brett cut the engine. He turned to her for a moment, the tension thick between them. "His body should be safe out here until we get your son back."

Willow bit down on her lip as the full implications of what they were doing hit her. Not only was she compromising evidence and disposing of a body, but when the truth was revealed, she would look like a bitter ex-wife—one who might have killed Leo and then called an old boyfriend to help her dispose of his body.

She could go to jail and so could Brett.

It would also drive a bigger wedge between him and his brother Maddox.

But what other choice did she have?

She touched the knot on the back of her head where the intruder had hit her, then looked down at her cell phone, willing it to ring.

Poor little Sam must be terrified. Wondering where she was. Wanting to be home in his own bed.

Resigned, she reached for the door handle. "Let's get this done and pray the kidnapper calls tonight, then we can explain everything to Maddox."

Brett's eyes flashed with turmoil at the mention of his brother, compounding her guilt. The men had just buried their beloved father and now she was asking *this* of him.

She hated herself for that.

But Sam's face flashed in her mind, and she couldn't turn back.

"WAIT IN THE TRUCK," Brett told Willow.

Brett jumped out of the pickup, walked to the truck bed and retrieved a shovel. Yanking on work gloves, he strode to a flat stretch between two boulders, a piece of land hidden from view and safe from animals scavenging for food.

A coyote howled in the distance and more night sounds broke the quiet. His breath puffed out as he jammed the shovel in the hard dirt and began to dig. Pebbles and dry dirt crunched, and he looked up to see Willow approaching with a second shovel.

"I told you to stay in the truck."

"This is my mess," Willow said. "I...have to help."

Brett wanted to spare her whatever pain he could. "Let me do it for you, Willow, *please*."

Her gaze met his in the dim light of the moon, and she shook her head, then joined him and together they dug the grave.

It took them over an hour to make a hole deep enough to cover Leo so the animals wouldn't scavenge for him. Willow leaned back against a boulder, her breath ragged. She looked exhausted, dirty and sweaty from exertion, and shell-shocked from the events of the night.

He returned to the truck, dragged Leo's body inside the rug from the bed, then hauled him over his shoulder and carried him to the grave. Before he dumped him inside, he retrieved a large piece of plastic from his trunk and placed it in the hole to protect the body even more.

Willow watched in silence as he tossed Leo into the grave, then he shoveled the loose dirt back on top of him, covering him with the mound until he was hidden from sight.

But he had a bad feeling that even though Leo was covered, Willow would still continue seeing his face in her mind.

He smoothed down the dirt, then stroked her arm. "It's done. Now we wait on the ransom call."

She nodded, obviously too numb and wrung out to talk, and he led her back to the truck. He tossed the shovels in the truck bed, grabbed a rag and handed it to Willow to wipe her hands.

She looked so shaken that he decided not to take her back to that house. There were a couple of small cabins on the north side of the ranch that weren't in use because they'd reserved that quadrant to build more stables. Even though he was a bull rider, he also did trick riding, so his father had wanted Brett to handle the horse side of the business. But when Brett left town, Maddox and his father had put the idea on hold. "I'm going to take you to one of the cabins to get some rest."

Willow didn't argue. Her hand trembled as she fastened her seat belt, then she leaned her head back and closed her eyes. He drove across the property to the north, where he hoped to find an empty cabin.

Five minutes later, he found the one he was looking for just a few feet from the creek. He parked and walked around to help Willow out. The door to the place was unlocked—so like the McCullens. Trustworthy to a fault.

The electricity was on, thank goodness, and

the place was furnished, although it was nothing fancy, but the den held a comfortable-looking sofa and chair and a double bed sat in the bedroom, complete with linens. He and Willow had sneaked out to this cabin years ago to make love in the afternoon.

Her eyes flickered with recognition for a moment before despair returned.

"Thank you for coming tonight," Willow said in a raw whisper.

He gestured toward the bedroom. "Get some rest. I'll hang around for a while."

She looked down at her hands, still muddy from the dirt and blood. "I have to wash up first."

He ducked into the bathroom and found towels and soap. The place was also fairly clean as if someone had used it recently. His father was always taking someone in to help them out so he wasn't surprised.He still felt like he'd walk into the main house and find him sitting in his chair. But he was gone.

Willow flipped on the shower, then reached for the button on her shirt to undress.

It was too tempting to be this close to her and not touch her, so he stepped into the hall and shut the door to give her some privacy. Self-doubts over his actions tonight assailed him, and he went to his truck, grabbed a bottle of whiskey and brought it inside.

As much as he wanted to comfort Willow and

hold her tonight, he couldn't touch her. She'd only called him to help her find her son.

And he would do that.

But tonight the stench of her husband's dead body permeated his skin, and the lies he would have to tell his brother haunted him.

IMAGES OF DIGGING her husband's grave tormented Willow as she showered. No matter how hard she scrubbed, she couldn't erase them.

Leo was dead. Shot. Murdered.

And Sam was missing.

Her little boy's face materialized, and her chest tightened. Sam liked soccer and climbing trees and chocolate chip cookies. And he had just learned to pedal on his bike with training wheels. Only Leo had run over his bike.

Where was Sam now? Was he cold or hungry?

She rinsed, dried off and looked at the clock. It was after four. Was Sam asleep somewhere, or was he too terrified to sleep? His favorite stuffed dinosaur was still in his room…

She found a robe in the closet and tugged it on, then checked her phone in case she'd missed the kidnapper. But no one had called.

Tears burned the backs of her eyelids. Why hadn't they phoned?

Nerves on edge, she walked into the kitchen and spotted a bottle of whiskey on the counter. Brett had always liked brown whiskey. In fact, in high school, he'd sneaked some of his father's to this very cabin and they'd imbibed before they'd made love.

She couldn't allow herself to think about falling in bed with Brett again.

This was an expensive brand of whiskey, though, much more so than the brand Joe McCullen drank. Of course, Brett had done well on the rodeo circuit.

Both financially and with the women.

An empty glass sat beside the bottle, and she poured herself a finger full, then found Brett sitting in the porch swing with a tumbler of his own.

He looked up at her when she stepped onto the porch, his handsome face strained with the night's events.

"I should go home," Willow said from the doorway.

Brett shook his head. "Not tonight. We'll pick up some of your things tomorrow, but you aren't staying in that house until this is over and Leo's killer is dead or in jail."

"But—"

"No buts, Willow." He sipped his whiskey. "It's not safe. Besides, we shouldn't disturb anything in the house, so when we do call Maddox in, he can process the place for evidence."

He was right. "I realize this is putting you in a difficult position with Maddox."

Brett shrugged. "That's nothing new."

Willow sank onto the swing beside him. She'd never had siblings although she'd always wanted a sister or a brother, especially when she was growing up. Her mother had died when she was five, and she'd been left with her father who'd turned to drinking to drown his problems. That alcohol had finally killed him two weeks before she'd graduated from high school.

Another reason she'd gravitated toward Brett and it had hurt so much when he'd left town. She had literally been alone.

"I know you've had issues, Brett, but your father just died, and you and your brothers should be patching things up." She took a swallow of her own liquor, grateful for the warmth of the alcohol as it eased her nerves. "Family means everything, Brett. When you don't have one anymore, you realize how important it is."

Brett's gaze latched with hers, but the flirtatious gleam she'd seen years ago and in the tabloids was gone. Instead, a dark intensity made his eyes look almost black.

"I'm sorry you lost yours. I know that last year with your dad was rough."

It was Willow's turn to shrug, although it was Brett leaving a second time that had sent her into Leo's arms. Made her vulnerable to his false charm.

"My family is Sam now. I can't go on if something happens to him."

Brett reached out and covered her hand with his. "We will find him, I promise. And I'll make sure whoever abducted him pays."

She desperately wanted to believe him.

"There's something I have to ask you, Willow."

A knot seized her stomach at his tone. "What?"

"Where were you earlier today?"

Willow tensed. "Why? You don't think *I* shot Leo, do you?"

He hesitated, long enough to make her think that he had considered the possibility. That hurt.

"No," he finally said. "But I have to ask, because the police will."

Willow sucked in a sharp breath. "I did errands, had to drop off some of my orders. Sam was staying with my neighbor Gina, but apparently Leo picked him up." That sick feeling hit her again.

"This other woman can corroborate your story?"

Willow pinched her lips together, angry. "Yes, Brett."

Would she need a more solid alibi to prove that she hadn't killed her husband?

THE PAIN IN Willow's eyes made Brett strengthen his resolve to help her. "Do you have any idea who abducted Sam?"

She shook her head, her hair falling like a

curtain around her face. "I didn't recognize the man's voice. And he wore a ski mask."

"You said that Leo didn't have a bank account? Where did he keep his money?"

Willow traced her finger along the rim of her glass. "He kept cash in a safe when he lived with me. But he cleaned that out when he left."

"It seems odd that a businessman wouldn't have had bank accounts, maybe even a financial advisor."

"I thought so, too, but he just got defensive every time I mentioned it."

Brett rocked the swing back and forth with his feet. "Where did he go when he moved out?"

"I don't know."

"He didn't send child support?"

"No. And I was okay with that. When he left, I was so glad to have him out of my life, out of Sam's life, that I didn't want anything from him."

Brett willed his temper in check. The McCullen men had been raised to protect women, and to honor them. No man ever laid a hand on a woman or child.

"How bad was it?" he asked gruffly.

Willow sighed wearily. "At first it was just arguments. He wanted to control everything, from the money I spent, to how I took care of the house. I stood my ground, and he didn't like it."

"Good for you."

A small smile tilted her mouth. "He was nice

in the beginning, Brett, but he changed once we married. Nothing I did was right. And he was always traveling and refused to tell me where he was going."

"You think he was having an affair?"

Willow shrugged. "It wouldn't have surprised me."

Brett contemplated that idea. What if Leo had been seeing another woman and she had killed him?

Still, why would that woman abduct Sam?

Unless she thought Willow had Leo's money.

"Tell me about his business," Brett said. "What did Leo do for a living?"

"When we first met, he said he'd made it big with some investment, something about mining uranium."

Made sense. Wyoming was rich in rare earth elements and mining.

"Did he say how much money he made? Thousands? A million?"

Willow bit down on her lip. "No. He just said he'd—we'd—be taken care of for life."

Brett considered the small house where Willow lived. "If he had so much money, why were you living in that little place?"

Willow frowned. "I moved there after Leo left. I wanted a fresh start."

"Where was your other house?"

"Cheyenne," Willow said. "But it was a rental,

too. He said he was holding out to buy a big spread and build his dream house. But he never started anything."

"Did he have a business card? Or was there a business associate he mentioned?"

"No." Willow's voice cracked. "I'm sorry. I'm not being much help."

She obviously hadn't known much about her husband, which seemed odd to him. Willow had always been honest, trusting, and she valued family but she was also cautious because her father had had problems.

So why had she been charmed by Leo? Had his money appealed to her?

That also didn't fit with the Willow he'd known.

"Did Leo have any family? A sister? Brother? Parents?"

"No," Willow said. "He lost both his parents." Willow leaned against the back of the porch swing, her face ashen. "Looking back, Brett, I feel like I didn't know Leo at all."

Brett tossed back the rest of his whiskey. "You're exhausted now, but maybe tomorrow you'll remember more."

If he was lucky, he'd find something in the house to add insight into Willow's dead husband.

Knowing more about him might clue them in to the reason for his death.

He patted Willow's hand. "Go inside and try to get some sleep."

"How can I sleep when I don't know where Sam is? He must be scared…and what if he's hurt? What if that man did something to him?"

Brett cupped her face with his hands. "Listen to me, Willow. If this man wanted something from Leo, and he didn't get it, he's going to use Sam as leverage. So if we figure out what kind of trouble Leo was in, we can figure out how to save your son."

He coaxed her to stand. "Try to rest until he calls with his demands."

Willow glanced down at his hand. "Are you staying here?"

He wanted to. But that would be too tempting.

"No. I'll run back to the farmhouse to shower. I'll bring you some breakfast in a little while, then we can stop by your house for some of your things."

He opened the door and ushered her inside. "Now lock up. You'll be safe here. And when the kidnapper calls, phone me and I'll come right over."

Her golden eyes flickered with fear, but she nodded and slipped inside. He waited until he heard the door lock, then hurried to his truck before he went inside and crawled in bed with her.

Tension thrummed through him as he drove back to the farmhouse and parked.

Just as he let himself inside the house, Maddox was jogging down the steps. His gaze roved over Brett's dirt-stained clothes, a disapproving scowl stretching his mouth into a thin line.

"We just buried our father, and you went out partying, huh?" Maddox muttered. "Some things never change, do they?"

Brett bit his tongue to keep from a retort.

Unable to tell him the truth, he let his brother believe the lesser of the evils, pasted on a cocky grin like he would after an all-night drunk and climbed the steps to his old room.

If his brother knew that he'd buried a murdered man on McCullen land, he'd lock him up and never talk to him again.

Chapter Six

Too on edge to sleep, Brett showered, anxious to wash the stench of Leo's dead body off him.

But all the soap in the world couldn't erase the memory of what he'd done.

He envisioned the headlines—Rodeo Star Brett McCullen Arrested for Covering Up a Murder, for Tampering with Evidence in a Homicide…

The list could go on and on.

If—no, *when*—it was revealed that he and Willow shared a past, people might think that the two of them had plotted to kill her husband so they could be together.

Perspiration beaded on his neck as he buttoned his shirt.

The only way to make sure the two of them weren't charged was to find out who had killed Leo. Then they could recover Willow's little boy and turn the situation over to Maddox.

He dressed in jeans, fastened his belt and yanked on his cowboy boots. Then he packed a duffel bag of clothes in case he needed to stay with Willow and stowed them in his Range Rover.

His eyes felt bleary from lack of sleep, but he couldn't rest right now. He had to find some answers.

Willow and her little boy were depending on him.

The first place he would start was Leo's truck. It had been left in Willow's drive. Maybe there was something inside it that would give him a lead.

The scent of strong coffee and bacon wafted through the air as he entered the dining room. Mama Mary was humming a gospel song in the kitchen, but she had set out coffee and juice along with hot biscuits, bacon and eggs on the side-board.

He poured himself a mug of coffee, then made a breakfast sandwich and wolfed it down. She ambled in just as he was finishing, her eyes probing his.

"How you doing this morning, Mr. Brett?"

He and his brothers always said Mama Mary had eyes in the back of her head, and a sixth sense that told her when one of them had been bad. She was giving him that look this morning.

He shrugged. "Okay."

"Hmm-hmm."

If guilt wasn't pressing against his chest so badly he would have chuckled. "It's hard being back here without Dad," he said, hoping she'd think his grief was all that was eating at him.

"I know. We're all gonna miss your daddy." She patted his shoulder and poured him another cup of coffee. "Best remember that and take care to make up with the ones still on this side of the ground."

He understood her not-so-subtle message.

Unfortunately his actions the night before would only create a bigger chasm and garner more disapproval from his older brother. He never could measure up to Maddox.

She cleared his plate. "Maddox wanted to check the fence on the west side before he went to the sheriff's office."

How Maddox handled being in the office and the ranch was beyond Brett. But then again, Maddox was the one who *could* do it all and make it look easy at the same time.

Hadn't his father told him that a million times?

"You know Maddox got engaged to this pretty lady named Rose?" Mama Mary said with a sparkle in her eye.

Brett nodded. "Is that her name?"

"Yeah, she's a sweetheart. Owns the antique store in town where Willow sells her quilts. Poor Rose had some trouble a while back, but Maddox handled it for her."

"I'm sure he did." He didn't mean to sound surly, but his tone bordered on sarcastic.

Mama Mary gave him a chiding look, and he grabbed one of the to-go mugs on the sideboard, filled it with coffee, wrapped an extra biscuit and bacon in a napkin for Willow and gave Mama Mary a peck on the cheek.

"Thanks for breakfast. I haven't had biscuits like that since I left here."

She grinned with pride, and he hurried away before she asked him where he was going. He could lie to Maddox, but it was harder to lie to Mama Mary because she could see right through him.

Wind stirred dust around his boots, and the temperature had dropped twenty degrees overnight. As he drove across the ranch, the beauty of the land struck him along with memories of riding with his brothers as a kid. The campouts and cattle drives. The horseshoe contests and trick riding.

When he'd left Pistol Whip, he'd been young and eager for travels, to see new places, to escape the routine of ranch life, and he'd enjoyed the different towns and women.

This morning, though, the land looked peaceful. The women's faces a blur.

There was only one woman he'd ever really cared about, and that was Willow.

By the time he reached her place, worry for her son dominated his mind.

Knowing Willow must be frantic, he scanned

the outside of her rental house and the property when he arrived. Everything appeared as he'd left it the night before.

Leo's truck was still parked on the lawn, the little boy's bike mangled.

He yanked on a pair of work gloves to keep from leaving fingerprints, then climbed out and walked over to the truck. For a man who supposedly had landed a windfall, the truck was old and shabby looking. Barring a few tools, the truck bed was empty.

The door to the cab was unlocked, as if the man had gotten out in a hurry. Brett slipped inside and checked the seat. Nothing.

No papers, computer or cell phone. No gun.

He opened the glove compartment and found a wallet with a driver's license and a hundred dollars in cash.

He didn't find an insurance card, but found a tiny slip of paper with a name and phone number.

It was a woman's name. Doris Benedict.

Brett's instincts kicked in. If Leo had another woman on the side, maybe she'd killed him.

He jammed the paper in his pocket. It was a place to start.

WILLOW DOZED TO SLEEP but dreamed of her little boy and Brett, and woke up in a sweat.

In the dream, Sam looked so much like his father sitting on that horse that it nearly took her breath away and resurrected memories of watching Brett at the rodeo when he was eighteen.

She'd fallen in love with him that day. He'd looked so handsome with his thick hair glinting in the sunlight. When he'd turned his flirtatious smile on her, she hadn't been able to resist.

She had been alone so long. Dubbed poor white trash because her father had been a mean drunk and she was motherless. The very reason she'd been determined to be a good mother to Sam.

But now he was missing because she'd been fooled by Leo's promises and wound up marrying a mean drunk herself.

But that day Brett had made her feel so special…not like poor trash. All the other girls at the rodeo wanted Brett McCullen, the up-and-coming rodeo star.

But after he'd received his buckle for winning, he'd walked over to her and kissed her right in front of the crowd.

How could she *not* have fallen in love with him?

It didn't matter.

Brett hadn't wanted her the past few years. He had plenty of women. And he certainly didn't intend to stay in Pistol Whip and settle down.

She had done the right thing. If she'd told Brett she was pregnant five years ago, he might have stuck around, but he would have resented her. And that would have destroyed their love.

She found some coffee in the kitchen and brewed a pot, then carried a mug and her phone to the front porch and sat down, praying it would ring with news about how to get Sam back.

BRETT DROVE BACK to the cabin, anxious to check on Willow. Hopefully the kidnapper would phone today with his demands.

But if Willow didn't have the money, what did they want?

Willow was sitting on the porch, sipping coffee and looking so damn lost and pained that his lungs squeezed for air. He'd do anything to make her happy again.

But the only way to do that was to put her son back in her arms.

He parked, then carried the biscuit in one hand as he walked up to the porch.

He handed her the food. "Any word?"

She unwrapped the biscuit, although she rewrapped it as if she couldn't eat. That, and the desolate look in her eyes, told him all he needed to know.

"I searched Leo's truck and found a woman's name scribbled on a slip of paper. Doris Benedict. Do you know her?"

"No. Who is she?" Willow ran a hand through her hair, the wavy strands tangling as the wind picked them up and whipped them around her face. Winter was blowing in to Pistol Whip with its cold and gusty windstorms.

"I don't know," Brett said. "But maybe she knows something about Leo that can help us."

Willow rose from the porch swing, her face even more pale in the early morning light. "I'll go with you."

"Are you sure? We don't know what we'll find—what her relationship with Leo was."

"I don't care if they were lovers," Willow said staunchly. "I was done with Leo a long time ago. But if she can help us find Sam, I have to talk to her."

Brett gave a clipped nod. She'd been done with Leo a long time ago—had she *loved* him, though?

At one time he'd thought she loved *him*. But when he'd left town, she'd completely cut him out of her life.

She disappeared inside the cabin and returned a moment later with her purse over her shoulder. But she kept her phone clutched in one hand. Her fingers were wrapped so tightly around it that they looked white.

She didn't look at him as she started down the steps. "Let's go."

Brett followed her, climbed in the truck and started the engine, the tension between them thick with unanswered questions as he drove toward the woman's address.

Doris Benedict lived in Laramie, in a stone

duplex on the outskirts of town. Dry scrub brush and weeds choked the tiny yard. No children's toys outside, so she must not have kids. Although the duplex didn't look fancy or expensive, a fairly new dark green sedan sat in the drive.

Brett and Willow walked together to the front door. Willow folded her arms while he buzzed the doorbell. A car engine rumbled from next door while voices from another neighbor herding her kids out to the bus stop echoed in the wind.

He punched the doorbell again, and a woman's voice shouted from inside that she was coming. A second later, the door opened, and a young woman with a bad dye job and sparkling earrings that dangled to her shoulders stood on the other side.

He guessed her age to be about thirty-four, although she had the ruddy skin of a heavy smoker, so she could have been younger.

Her flirtatious smile flitted over him. "You're that rodeo star?"

He nodded. "Yes, ma'am. Brett McCullen."

When her gaze roved from him to Willow, her ruby-red lips formed a frown. "What do you want?"

Brett narrowed his eyes at the contempt in her voice.

"My name is Willow James, um Willow Howard—"

"I know who you are." Doris reached for the

door as if to slam it in their faces, but Brett caught it with one hand.

Willow looked stunned. "How do you know me?"

Doris removed a cigarette from the pack in the pocket of her too-tight jeans. "Leo married you."

Brett frowned. "How do you know Leo, Ms. Benedict?"

The woman angled her face toward him, her eyes menacing. "He and I dated a while back."

"How far back?" Brett asked.

She lit her cigarette, tilted her head back and inhaled a drag, then glared at Willow. "About five years. I thought we were going to get hitched, but then he married you."

"You dated Leo?" Willow asked.

The woman pushed her face toward Willow. "What's that supposed to mean? You don't think he'd go out with a woman like me?"

"It's not that," Willow said quickly. "It's just that Leo never mentioned his prior relationships."

Doris chuckled. "Honey, there's a lot of things Leo didn't tell you."

Willow's breath rasped out. "Like what?"

Doris blew smoke into the air. "Why don't you ask him?"

Willow glanced at him and he gave a short shake of his head, silently willing her not to divulge that Leo was dead. Not yet.

"When was the last time you saw him?" Brett asked.

Doris shrugged. "About a month ago."

"You were seeing him while he was married to Willow?" Brett asked.

Doris poked him in the chest. "Don't judge me, Brett McCullen. Leo loved me."

"Then why did he marry me?" Willow asked.

Doris laughed again. "Because you were respectable. And Leo needed a respectable wife so nobody in town would ask too many questions."

"Why didn't he want them asking questions?" Brett asked.

Doris tapped ashes on the porch floor at Willow's feet. "Again—why don't you ask him?"

"Because I'm asking you," Willow said, her voice stronger. "You obviously don't like me and wanted Leo for yourself. So when I filed for divorce, did he come to you?"

Doris's eyes widened in shock. "You were divorcing Leo?"

Brett scrutinized her body language. She sounded sincerely surprised. But if she'd discovered he and Willow weren't together, and he still didn't want her, she might have killed him out of anger.

Although she didn't appear to be the motherly type. So if she had killed Leo, why kidnap Sam?

SAM HUGGED THE RAGGEDY stuffed animal under his arm and rubbed his eyes. He wanted his mommy.

But he remembered what had happened the night before and tears filled his eyes. Those bad men...two of them. One with the scarf over his mouth and the other with that black ski mask.

All he could see was their eyes. Mean eyes.

And the tattoo. Both of them had tattoos on their necks. One had a long rattlesnake that wound around his throat. The other had crossbones like he'd seen on some of the T-shirts at Halloween.

Those crossbones meant poison or the devil or something else evil.

Just like the bad men.

Red flashed behind his eyes, and he heard the gunshots blasting like fireworks. He covered his ears to snuff them out just like he'd done at his house.

But he'd peeked from the closet and seen his daddy and all that blood ran down his shirt. Then Daddy's eyes had gone wide, like they did on TV when someone was dead.

He didn't much care if he was dead, and he felt real bad about that. Kids were supposed to love their fathers. But he couldn't help it—his daddy had been mean to his mommy.

He didn't want to be dead, too, though.

He sat up on the cot and pushed the curtain to the side and looked through the dirty window. A spider was crawling across the windowsill, and a tree branch was beating against the glass.

He tried to see where he was, but all he saw was woods.

Big trees stuck together, so close that he couldn't see past them or even between them for a path.

He pushed at the window to open it and climb out. He was scared of the woods and the dark, but he'd rather run in there than be stuck here with these bad men with the tattoos and guns.

But the window wouldn't move. He pushed and shoved. Then he saw nails. They were hammered in the edge to keep it closed.

His chin quivered. They had locked him in here, and he was never going to get out.

Footsteps pounded outside the door, and he dropped back onto the bed, rolled to his side, grabbed the blanket and pulled it over him, then pretended to be asleep.

The door screeched open, then the snake-man's voice said, "What are we gonna do with the kid?"

"Dump him when we get what we want."

Sam pressed his hand over his mouth to keep from crying out loud.

Their boots pounded harder. They were coming toward him.

He squeezed his eyes shut, swallowing hard

not to let the tears fall. Then one of them jerked the blanket off his head.

"Say *hi* to your mother, kid," Snake man said.

Sam couldn't help it. A tear slid down his cheek. Then the big man snapped a picture of him with his phone.

A second later, he tossed the blanket back to him, then stalked across the room. The big man's words echoed in his head.

They were calling his mommy. Maybe she'd come and get him.

But they said something else. They were going to dump him when they got what they wanted. Would he ever see his mommy again?

Chapter Seven

Willow couldn't take her eyes off Doris.

Leo had been involved with *this* woman?

Doris was the complete opposite of her. Everything from her low-cut top to those red high-heel boots screamed that she liked the wilder side of life.

She'd considered the fact that during their marriage Leo had cheated on her. He was a womanizer and liked to flirt. And he'd lost interest in her early on, almost as soon as they'd exchanged vows.

But now she realized he and Doris had rolled in the hay while Willow had wondered what was wrong with her, if she didn't possess enough sex appeal to please him.

She certainly hadn't had enough to keep Brett in town. He'd wanted other women, too.

But Doris said Willow had been a tool to make Leo look good. For what reason?

Who had he wanted to impress?

And if Doris had killed Leo, why had she admitted that she knew *her*?

"Can we come inside for a minute?" Willow asked. "I need to use your restroom." What she really needed was to know if Sam was inside the house.

Doris glared at her, but waved them inside the foyer. "First door on the left."

Willow hurried down the hall, but she did a quick visual as she passed the small living room. Basic furniture, hair and makeup magazines on the oak coffee table, but no toys or children's books.

She ducked in the bathroom and closed the door, then checked the closet and cabinet. Sam wasn't hidden inside, and there were no kids' toothpaste or toys. She flushed the toilet, so as not to draw suspicion, then ran some water in the sink. When she finished, she slipped out and peered into the kitchen. Doris was handing Brett a cup of coffee.

She tiptoed down the hall to the bedrooms. One on the left that looked ostentatious with a hot-pink satin comforter, a silk robe tossed across a chaise and a door that probably led to a master bath. She veered into the second bedroom, which was filled with junk. Boxes of items Doris had obviously ordered online. She didn't see any signs of Sam or a child anywhere, though. She checked the closet and found more boxes stacked, many of them unopened. Many from expensive department stores.

How does the woman support her shopping habit?

Brett's voice echoed as she made her way back to him.

"Where were you yesterday, Doris?" Brett asked.

Doris tapped cigarette ashes into a coffee cup she held in her hand. "I was out. Why you want to know?"

"Out where?" Brett asked.

"Honey, you sound like a cop, not a cowboy"

Doris batted her lashes at Brett and traced a finger along his collar. Willow bit her lip. Surely Brett wouldn't be attracted to Doris like Leo had…

Brett winked at her, irking Willow even more. "Just indulge me, Doris," Brett said smoothly. "Were you with Leo?"

Anger flickered in the woman's eyes for a brief second. "No. I had to pull a double shift at Hoochies."

Willow inhaled to stem a reaction. Hoochies was a well-known bar where the waitresses offered dessert on the side.

"I suppose someone at Hoochies can verify that," Brett said.

Doris jerked her hand back. "You said that like I need a damn alibi."

Willow couldn't resist. She didn't like the fact that Leo cheated on her with this woman or that she'd touched Brett, and that Brett didn't seem to mind. "Maybe you do."

Panic tinged Doris's voice. "Did something happen to Leo?"

Willow shrugged. "Do you know anyone who'd want to hurt him?"

Doris took a step toward Willow. "Where is he? What happened? Is he hurt?"

For a millisecond, Willow almost felt sorry for the woman. Doris actually loved that lying bastard. "It's possible."

Doris grabbed Willow's arm. "What's that supposed to mean?"

Willow extracted herself from the woman's claws. "Just answer the question. Do you know anyone who'd want to hurt him?"

Doris glanced at Brett as if she wanted assurance that Leo was okay, but Brett maintained a straight face.

"Did he owe someone money?" Brett asked.

"Maybe." Doris's voice cracked. "I know he got in some trouble a while back."

"What kind of trouble?" Brett asked.

"Something with the law," Doris said in a low voice. "He never told me exactly what."

Willow grimaced. He'd certainly never shared that information with her either.

"And then there was his old man. The two of them didn't get along."

"His father?" Willow asked, her breath catching.

"Yeah," Doris said as she snatched another cigarette and lit up. "I don't know what happened between them, but there was some bad blood."

Willow forced herself not to react. Leo had claimed both his parents were dead.

Was everything he'd told her a lie?

BRETT SCHOOLED HIS FACE into a neutral expression, although it was all he could do not to punch his fist through a wall.

How had a man like Leo won Willow's sweet heart?

And why would a man cheat on Willow with Doris, when Willow was the most beautiful, tenderhearted, desirable woman in the whole damn world?

"What was his father's name?" he asked.

Doris shrugged. "Hell, I don't know. Every time I tried to ask him, he got mad. Told me it was none of my business."

Brett shifted. He wished she'd give him something concrete. Although this could be a lead. If Leo had been in trouble before, especially with the law, he probably had an arrest record.

Another thought occurred to him. One of his

buddies had won thousands in the rodeo circuit, but he'd lost it all in Vegas.

"Was Leo into gambling?"

Doris inhaled and blew smoke into the air, her gaze fixed on him. "You're really scaring me now."

"Listen," Willow said. "Leo disappeared with my savings and I need it for medical expenses for my son."

Brett admired the way Willow told the lie without giving herself away. He watched Doris for a reaction, anything that might tip them off that she knew where Sam was being held.

"I have no idea where Leo is," Doris said instead. "But if I talk to him, I'll tell him about the kid." Her voice grew low, almost sincere. "I hope it's not too serious."

Willow gave a little shake of her head, but real tears glittered on her eyelashes.

"Was he into gambling?" Brett asked. "It could explain the reason he stole from Willow."

"He gambled some, but I don't think he was in big debt for it, if that's what you mean."

"Did he leave any money with you?"

Doris muttered a sarcastic sound. "If he left me money, do you think I'd be living in this dump or working doubles at Hoochies?"

Good point.

Brett crossed his arms. "Did Leo have any friends he might have been staying with?"

"You mean female friends?" She gave Willow a condescending look. "If he had other women, I didn't know about it. Then again, I never thought he'd marry *you*."

Brett cleared his throat. "How about male friends?"

"You mean friends who'd let him hide out with them?" Doris asked with a sarcastic grunt.

Brett nodded.

She stared at the burning tip of her cigarette for a long minute as if in thought. "He mentioned this guy named Gus a while back. But I don't know where he is. I think he might have been in jail."

Brett's instincts kicked in. If Leo and this guy were friends, they might have been in cahoots over something illegal.

He wasn't a cop, but his brother was. He wanted to ask Maddox for his help more than he'd ever wanted to ask him anything in his life.

But the tears Willow had just wiped away haunted him. He couldn't turn to his brother now, not as the sheriff.

Although, if he could use Maddox's computer, he could research Leo's past. His father, his arrest record, this man, Gus…

That information might lead him to whatever Leo was involved in that had gotten him killed.

And then to Willow's son.

"Thank you, Doris." Brett handed her a card

with his number on it. "If you think of anything else that might help us find Leo, let me know."

Doris caught his arm before he could leave, but she looked at Willow as she spoke. "If you hear from him, tell him I'm still here."

He expected Willow to show a spark of jealousy, but she gave Doris a pitying look and walked back to the car.

Brett followed, his mind ticking away. First they'd stop by Willow's house for her to pack a bag, then they'd go back to Horseshoe Creek.

Maybe he could sneak onto Maddox's home computer and access his police databases while Maddox was out.

WILLOW CHECKED HER PHONE as Brett drove away from Doris's. "Why haven't they called?"

Brett made the turn onto the highway leading back toward her rental house. "They're probably putting together a list of their demands."

She prayed they were. Although she had no idea what they would want from her. She had a couple of thousand in the bank, but that was all.

"Do you think Doris was telling the truth?" Brett asked.

Willow sighed. "She didn't seem to know Leo was dead. If she had, why wouldn't she have hidden the fact that she knew me?"

"She was pretty up-front about that," Brett

agreed. "Did you see anything in the house to indicate Sam was there or had been there?"

Willow shook her head no. "If Doris didn't murder Leo, who did?"

"That's what we're going to find out. I think the key is somewhere in Leo's past."

Willow heaved a breath. "I feel like such a fool, Brett. I thought I knew Leo when I first met him, but I didn't know him at all."

"He showed you what he wanted you to see," Brett said.

Humiliation washed over Willow. She'd made such a mess out of her life, while Brett had risen to success. "It's my fault Sam is missing," she said, her chest aching with guilt. "If anything happens to him…"

Brett squeezed her hand. "Nothing is going to happen to him. If he's anything like his mom, he's a tough little guy."

He was nothing like her and everything like Brett. But she bit back that comment for now. When they found Sam, she'd have to tell Brett the truth.

For now…she needed him focused and helping her. Because if he knew Sam was his, he'd blame her, too. And she couldn't bear any more guilt.

They lapsed into silence until they reached her house, and Brett parked. Leo's truck was still sitting in the drive, Sam's mangled bike beneath it. She gritted her teeth as they walked up to the front door. "Just pack a bag with some clothes. You can stay at the cabin until this is over."

The scent of blood and death permeated the air as Willow entered the house, then her bedroom. The bloodstain that had seeped through the sheets to the mattress looked even more stark in the daylight.

She rushed to the closet, grabbed an overnight bag, then threw a couple of pairs of jeans, a loose skirt, some blouses and underwear inside. In the bathroom she gathered her toiletries and makeup, then carried the bag back to the hall. Brett was kneeling in front of Sam's room with a dark look on his face.

"What is it?" Willow asked.

He gestured toward the floor. "A bloodstain. It looks like Leo might have initially been shot here, then moved to the bed."

"Why move him to the bed?"

"Perhaps to frame you."

Perspiration beaded on Willow's hand. "And when the police learn that Leo had another woman, they'll assume I killed him out of jealousy."

"It's possible. All the more reason we uncover the truth first."

Willow glanced up from the stain and into Sam's room. Horror washed over her as she realized that Sam could have easily seen Leo being gunned down from his room.

Poor Sam. What would witnessing a cold-blooded murder do to a four-year-old?

And if the killer knew that Sam could identify him, he might not let her have him back even if she did pay the ransom…

Chapter Eight

"Willow?" Brett gently touched her arm. "Are you all right?"

She blinked back tears. "How can I be all right when my little boy is in the hands of a murderer? What if they've hurt him, Brett?"

Brett made a low sound in his throat. "Don't think like that, Willow. We'll find him, I promise."

She nodded, although the fear was almost paralyzing. Finally, though, she stood and went into Sam's room. For a moment, she was frozen in place at the sight of his stuffed dinosaur and the soccer ball and the blocks on the floor. The top to his toy chest stood open, a few of his trucks and cars still inside although several of the toys had been pulled out and lay across the floor.

She ran her finger over the quilt she'd made for Sam. He'd picked out the dark green fabric because it was the color of grass, and he'd asked for horses on the squares. She'd appliquéd them on the squares, then sewed them together for him just a few months ago.

Would he ever get to sleep under that quilt again?

"We should go," Brett said in a deep voice. "I want to use Maddox's computer while he's at his office and see what I can learn about Leo and that man, Gus."

Willow grabbed Sam's dinosaur and the throw he liked, a plush brown one with more horses on it, and clutched them to her. Brett carried her overnight bag, and she followed him outside to his truck.

Sam's sweet little-boy scent enveloped her as she pressed the dinosaur to her cheek, and emotions welled inside her. Last week they'd talked about Christmas and finding a tree to cut down on their own this year. They'd planned to decorate using a Western-themed tree with horse and farm-animal ornaments, since Sam was infatuated by the ranches nearby.

If only he knew his father lived on a spread like Horseshoe Creek, and that he was a rodeo star...

One day, maybe. Although, Sam might hate her for lying to him about his father.

BRETT PARKED AT the ranch house, grateful Maddox's SUV was gone and Mama Mary's Jeep wasn't in the drive. She usually liked to grocery shop or visit friends from the church in the morning or early afternoon, but came home in plenty of time to make supper.

Maddox had another cook who prepared food for the ranch hands, and a separate dining hall for them to eat, as well.

He had no idea where Ray was. He'd made himself scarce since the funeral, probably biding his time until the reading of the will, after which he could head out of town.

"I'm sorry for taking you away from your family," Willow said. "I know this is a difficult time for you and your brothers, and you need to be spending time with them."

He hated to admit it, but he hadn't thought much about them since Willow's panicked phone call. "Don't worry about us. Our problems have nothing to do with you." Except of course, Maddox would disagree when he discovered Brett was covering up a murder, and he'd buried Willow's husband on McCullen land. Land as sacred to Maddox as it had been to Joe McCullen.

His conversation with his father about Willow having trouble echoed in his head, and he wondered if his dad had known more about Leo than he'd revealed.

The sound of cattle and horses in the distance took some of the edge off Brett's emotions as he and Willow walked up to the house. "You didn't eat your breakfast," Brett said. "I'm sure Mama Mary left something for lunch."

Willow paused to watch a quarter horse galloping in the pasture. "I'm not really hungry, Brett."

"I know, but you have to keep up your strength. I'll get us something if you want to relax in the office."

She mumbled okay, then he ushered her to the corner table in the gigantic office their father shared with Maddox, while Brett hurried to the kitchen and found meat loaf sandwiches already prepared, as if Mama Mary remembered their high school days when the boys had worked the ranch and come in starved.

He poured two glasses of tea and carried them and the sandwiches to the office. Willow nibbled on hers, while he consumed his in three bites. Their father's computer was ancient, but Maddox had installed a new one for the ranch business, one he also used for work when he was out of the office.

He attempted to access police databases, but doing so required a password. He tried Maddox's birthday, then the name of Maddox's first pony and their first dog. None fit.

He stewed over it for a minute, then plugged in their father's birthday. Bingo.

Determined to find answers for Willow, he punched Leo's name into the system. DMV records showed he had a current driver's license, then Brett ran a background check.

"Willow, listen to this. Leo Howard was born

to Janie and Hicks Howard thirty-two years ago, although Janie died when Leo was five. His father, Hicks, worked in a factory that made farm equipment, but he suffered debilitating injuries from a freak tractor accident on his own farm six years ago."

Willow nearly choked on the sandwich, and sipped her tea. "I still don't understand why he wouldn't tell me his father was alive."

"It's worth paying his father a visit to find out."

She wiped her mouth on a napkin and peered at the screen over his shoulder.

He ran a search for police records and watched as a photo of a man named Leo Stromberg, then Leo Hammerstein, popped up, both bearing Leo Howard's photo—both aliases.

Willow gasped. "Oh, my goodness. Leo had a police record."

"For stealing from his boss, a rancher named Boyle Gates, but apparently Gates dropped the charges." He scrolled farther. "But it says here he was implicated in a cattle-rustling operation. One of the men, Dale Franklin, was killed during the arrest. The other, Gus Garcia, is in prison serving time for the crime."

"How did Leo escape prison time?"

"Apparently Garcia copped to the crime. Although the police suspected a large cattle rustling operation, Garcia insisted that no one else except Franklin was involved. Franklin died in the arrest. Garcia is still in prison."

"You think he has something to do with Leo and Sam's disappearance?"

"That's what we're going to find out." Brett jotted down Garcia's full name, then the address for Leo's father. "First we'll pay a visit to Hicks Howard, then we'll go see Garcia."

An engine rumbled outside, then quieted, and Brett heard the front door open and slam. He flipped off the computer, ushered Willow over to the table and picked up his tea.

The door to the office screeched open, and Maddox filled the doorway, his broad shoulders squared, that air of superiority and disapproval radiating from him.

"What's going on here?"

Brett shrugged. "Willow stopped by to pay her condolences about Dad."

Maddox tipped his Stetson toward Willow in a polite greeting. "Hey, Willow. Nice to see you. How's your boy?"

Willow's eyes darkened with pain, but she quickly covered her emotions. "He's growing up fast."

Maddox smiled at her, but looked back at Brett. "You're having lunch in Dad's office?"

Brett shrugged and said the first thing that entered his head. "Thought I'd feel closer to Dad this way."

Maddox's brows quirked as if he didn't believe him, but Brett had spoken a half-truth. He did feel closer to his father in this room. He envisioned Joe resting in his big recliner with his nightly shot of bourbon, a book in his hand, his head lolling to the side as he nodded off.

Maddox gave him an odd look, then at least pretended to buy the lie. Brett was grateful for that.

But he picked up his and Willow's plates and tea glasses and carried them to the kitchen, anxious to leave.

The day was passing quickly, and he didn't want Willow to spend another night without her son.

EARLY AFTERNOON SUNLIGHT faded beneath the gray clouds as Brett maneuvered the long drive to Hicks Howard's farm. The place was miles from nowhere and looked as if it hadn't been operational in years. Run-down outbuildings, overgrown pastures and a muddy pond added to the neglected feel.

If Leo had come here, it had probably been to hide out. But if he was in trouble, whoever he'd crossed had found him anyway.

Willow checked her phone again, willing it to ring with some word on Sam. Why hadn't the kidnapper called yet?

Terrifying scenarios raced through her head,

but she forced herself to tune them out. She had to think positive, had to believe that she would bring Sam home.

Willow tensed, her chest hurting. Maybe she should tell Brett that Sam wasn't Leo's now. But...she wasn't ready for his reaction, for the anger, to explain why she'd kept her secret for so long.

Granted, she'd had her reasons. Brett had left her to sow his oats. He hadn't wanted to settle down. If he'd stayed around, he would have known about Sam.

Brett rolled to a stop beside a tractor overgrown by weeds. It looked as if it hadn't been used in a decade. A rusted pickup covered in mud sat under an aluminum shed.

As he approached, a mangy-looking gray cat darted beneath the porch of the wooden house. Boards were rotting on the floor, and the shutters were weathered, paint peeling.

Brett knocked on the door, and a noise sounded inside. Something banging, maybe a hammer. He knocked louder this time, and a minute later, the hammering stopped and a man yelled to hang on.

The door opened and a craggy, thin, balding man leaning on a walker stared up at them over wire-rimmed glasses. "If you're selling something, I don't want it."

"We're not selling anything. We just want to

talk." Brett gestured to Willow, and she introduced herself.

"Mr. Howard, I was married to your son, Leo."

"What?" The man grunted as he shifted his weight. "I hate to say it, honey, but you don't look like Leo's type." He raked his gaze up and down her body. "My son usually goes for the more showy girls."

Remembering Doris, she understood his point. "Did Leo tell you he was married?"

The older man scratched at the beard stubble on his chin. "No, but he didn't come around much."

"Why was that?" Brett asked.

Mr. Howard wrinkled his nose. "Why you folks asking about my son? Is he in some kind of trouble?"

"Would it surprise you if I said he was?" Brett asked.

"No. Leo was always messing up, skirting the law. From the time he was a teenager, he hated this farm. I was never good enough for him, never made enough money." He gestured at the walker and his bum leg. "When he left here, he said he was going to show me that he wasn't stupid like me. That he'd be rich one day."

"Was he?" Willow asked.

Howard shrugged. "About five years ago he came back with a duffel bag of money, all puffed up with himself. But when I asked him how he got it, he hem-hawed around."

"You thought he'd gotten it illegally?" Willow asked.

His head bobbed up and down. "I confronted him, and that's when he came at me." He gestured toward his leg. "That's how come I had my accident."

Willow's pulse hammered. Leo had caused his father's accident? No wonder he hadn't told her about him…

THE MORE BRETT learned about Leo Howard, the less he liked him. "Did he give you an indication as to how he got the money?"

"At first I thought he probably won it at the races, but when I was in the hospital after my leg got all torn up, the sheriff over in Rawlins stopped by and asked me if Leo stole some money from his boss. Some big hotshot rancher."

"Boyle Gates?"

"Yeah, I believe that was his name."

"Gates dropped the charges?" Brett asked.

Howard coughed. "Yeah. Don't ask me why, though."

Brett studied the old man. "You must have been angry at your son for the way he treated you."

"Like I said, he was trouble. I did all I could to help him, but it wasn't ever enough."

"Leo and I were separated for the past three years," Willow interjected. "Have you talked to him during that time?"

Howard shook his head no.

"Do you know any of his friends or men he worked with?"

"No, I think he was too ashamed of me to bring any of them around."

Or maybe he'd been too ashamed of his own friends, since they were probably crooks.

KNOWING THAT LEO had hurt his father made Willow feel ill. How had she not seen beneath his facade?

Family meant everything to her. Not money. But obviously Leo had wanted wealth and would use anyone in his path to obtain it.

Brett left his phone number in case the man thought of someone Leo might have contacted the past year.

"You didn't tell him that he has a grandson," Brett said as they settled back inside his truck.

Willow's heart pounded. She hated to keep lying to Brett, especially when he was helping her. But she needed to find the right moment to tell him the truth.

Suddenly her phone buzzed, and she quickly checked the number. *Unknown.* Fear and hope mingled as she punched Connect.

"Hello," Willow said in a choked whisper.

"You want to see your son again?"

"Yes. Please don't hurt him."

Brett covered her hand with his, so they were both holding the phone and he could hear. "We need proof that Sam is all right."

"I told you not to call the cops," the man shouted.

"He's not a cop," Willow said, panicked. "He's just a friend."

"You want to see your son alive, do what we say."

"I will, I promise. Just tell me what you want."

"The half million Leo stashed. We'll contact you with the drop."

Willow's stomach contracted. Leo had a half million dollars stashed somewhere?

"Let me speak to Sam," she whispered.

But the line clicked to silent. A second later, the phone dinged with a text.

Willow started to tremble as she looked at the image. It was a picture of Sam on a cot, clutching a raggedy blanket, tears streaming down his face.

Emotions overcame her and a sob wrenched from her throat. *Sam was alive.*

But he looked terrified, and she had no idea what money the man was talking about, or how to find it.

Chapter Nine

Willow pressed her hand to her mouth to keep from screaming.

Brett dragged her into his arms, and she collapsed against his chest, her body shaking with the horror of that photograph.

"*Shh*, it's going to be all right," Brett said in a low, gruff voice. "We'll find him, I swear."

Willow gulped as she dug her nails into his chest. "What kind of horrible person scares a child like that?"

Brett stroked her hair, his head against hers, as if he wanted to absorb her pain. He'd always acted tough, but he was tenderhearted and had confessed how much he'd hurt when he'd lost his mother. And now he'd lost his dad, and she was dumping on him.

If he knew Sam was his, he'd probably be hurting even more…

Maybe it was best she not tell him yet. They

needed to work together and if he was mad at her, that might be impossible.

Besides, when she brought Sam home and he grew attached to Brett, it would be even more difficult when Brett left town.

And he would return to the rodeo. Roaming and riding was in his blood.

He rocked her in his arms, and it had been so long since she'd been held and loved that she savored being close to him again. She had always loved Brett and had missed him so much.

Yet when this was over, Brett would go back to all those other women. If she let herself love him again, she might fall apart when he walked away. And she couldn't do that. She had to be strong for Sam.

Her heart in her throat, she forced herself to release him, then inhaled to gather her composure. She could still feel the tenderness in his arms and the worry in his voice.

He'd promised her he'd find Sam, but they both knew he might not be able to keep that promise. That the men who'd abducted Sam were very bad.

"Willow, did you know anything about Leo having a half million dollars?"

A sarcastic laugh bubbled in her throat. "Of course not. Like I said earlier, he claimed he'd made good money before we married, but I never saw it. He said he'd invested it and when the investment paid off, he was going to buy a big spread for us. But things fell apart shortly after the wedding." And now she realized he'd agreed only because he'd married her as a cover for himself.

Brett veered onto the road and drove away from the Howards' property. "What happened?"

Willow shrugged. She really didn't want to talk about Leo. Leo was the biggest mistake of her life.

"Willow, we were friends once. It might help if you told me."

Friends? He'd been the love of her life.

But right now she needed whatever he could give her. "Leo acted stressed all the time. *Secretive.* He left for days, sometimes weeks, at a time. And when I asked about his trips, he got angry and said he was trying to make it big. I…told him I didn't care about money, but he was obsessed."

"Just like his father said."

Willow nodded. She didn't care why Leo had stolen money or that he'd lied about his father.

All she cared about was who he'd angered enough to take her son.

BRETT STEERED THE TRUCK toward Rawlins, where the state prison was, hoping Gus Garcia had some answers.

He'd do anything to alleviate Willow's pain. Granted he didn't have a kid, but if he did, he'd be blind with fear right now.

And he'd kill anyone who tried to hurt his child.

Hell, he'd kill anyone who hurt Willow's child.

His phone buzzed, and he glanced at the caller ID display. His publicist and agent, Ginger Redman. Knowing she'd badger him to get back to work, he let it roll to voice mail.

"Aren't you going to answer that?" Willow asked.

"It's not important," Brett said and realized that for the first time in years, his career wasn't his top priority. He'd chased his dreams and become popular and had his picture taken a thousand times.

But he'd missed years with his father, he and his brothers were barely speaking, and he'd lost Willow to another man. They should have had a family together.

But…he'd had a wild streak and had to see what was out in the world.

He glanced at Willow and chewed the inside of his cheek. He had to admit he'd had a lot of women since he'd left Horseshoe Creek. Not as many as the tabloids reported, but enough so that he couldn't remember all their names or faces.

But the only one he'd ever cared about was the woman sitting in the seat next to him.

"Maybe Leo hid that money in his truck," Willow said, her lost expression tearing at him.

"I searched the truck and didn't find any money." Brett gave her a look of regret. "Can you think of anywhere else he'd hide it? Did he have a safety deposit box?"

Willow rubbed the space between her eyes as if she was thinking hard. "Not that I know of."

"How about a gym locker somewhere? Or an office where he could have had a safe?"

"No. But apparently, I was totally in the dark about what he was doing."

Brett hated the self-derision in her voice. "Willow, it sounds like he was a professional liar. You saw what he wanted you to see."

"So that makes me a big fool." Willow rubbed her forehead again. "What's worse is that I allowed him in Sam's life. I trusted him with my little boy, and now Sam's in danger because of my stupidity."

"It's not your fault," Brett said, as he made the turn onto the road leading to the prison.

"Yes it is. I'm his mother. It's my job to protect him and I failed."

"It was his father's job, as well, Willow. He's the one to blame."

Willow looked down at her hands, the wilderness stretching between them as desolate as the silence. Wind whistled through the car windows, signs of winter evident in the dry brush and brittle grass. Trees swayed in the gusty breeze, the wind tossing tumbleweed and debris across the road.

"Sam is afraid of storms," Willow said, her voice cracking.

"Just hang on," Brett said. "We'll find that money. And if we don't, I'll tap into my own resources."

Willow's eyes widened. "I know you've done well, Brett, but you don't have that kind of money, do you?"

Brett gulped. "Not half a million," he said. "But I can put together a hundred thousand. And if push comes to shove, I could sell Maddox my share of the ranch."

Willow's lip quivered, and he wanted to drag her into his arms. But he'd reached the drive to the prison and the security gate, so he squared his shoulders and pulled up to the guard's station, then reached for his ID.

EMOTIONS NEARLY OVERWHELMED WILLOW. Brett had offered to give her the money to save Sam, when he had no idea he was his own son.

Guilt choked her.

She should have told him about Sam. She should tell him now.

But…there was so much to discuss. And at the moment, they had to focus on finding Sam. Then she'd tell Brett everything.

And pray that he'd forgive her.

But would he want to stay around and be part of Sam's life? Or would he head back to his rodeo life with the groupies, late-night parties and the fame?

The guard requested their ID and asked who they'd come to visit, then recognized Brett and practically dove from his booth to shake his hand.

Willow tamped down her insecurities. Brett was a celebrity. She was a small-town mom who sold quilts for a living. They lived different lives now, lives that were too far apart for them to even consider a relationship.

The guard waved Brett through and must have radioed ahead, because when they reached the prison entrance, another guard greeted them with enthusiasm and the warden rushed to shake his hand. It took a few seconds to clear security, then the warden escorted them to his office.

"You want to see Gus Garcia?" The warden's tone was questioning. "May I ask why?"

She and Brett hadn't strategized, so she used the most logical story that came to mind. "I think he might have information about my husband," Willow said. "He left me and my son, and I'm trying to get child support."

"*Ahh*, I see." He motioned for the guard to take them to a visitor's room, and Willow and Brett followed the guard down the hall.

Barring a bare table and two straight chairs, the room was empty. A guard escorted Garcia inside, the inmate's handcuffs and shackles clanging as he walked. Willow's stomach quivered with nerves at the beady set to his eyes.

He was short and robust with a shaved head, a tattoo of a cobra on one arm, and scars on his arms and face. "Keep your hands where I can see them and no touching," the guard ordered.

The beefy man shoved Garcia into a chair, and Brett gestured for Willow to sit while he remained standing, his arms crossed, feet spread. His stance defied Garcia to start something.

"What do you want with me?" Garcia asked.

"My husband was Leo Howard," Willow began.

Garcia looked genuinely shocked. "Howard got married?"

"Yes," Willow said. "Five years ago."

Garcia chuckled. "That's a surprise."

Brett cleared his throat. "We need to know what happened between you and Howard and those other men the police suspected were working with you on that cattle-rustling ring." Brett hesitated, obviously studying Garcia's reaction. "You took the fall for them. Why?"

"Who the hell told you to come and talk to me?" Garcia's eyes darted sideways as if he thought he was being lured into a trap.

"Look, we don't care what you did," Brett said. "But we suspect that you were working with a group, and that Howard was involved. We also believe that Howard took the money you all made, and tried to cut your partners out of their share.

Anger slashed on Garcia's face, and he stood. "I don't know what you're talking about. Now, leave."

"Please," Willow said.

"I don't know where any money is." Garcia waved his handcuffs in the air. "How could I? I've been locked up in this hellhole."

"But Leo worked with you, didn't he?" Willow cried. "Did he promise you he'd keep your share if you took the fall?"

Garcia turned to leave, but Willow caught his arm. He froze, his body teeming with anger. The guard stepped forward, but Willow gave him a pleading look and the guard stepped back.

Willow lowered her voice. "Please, Mr. Garcia. I think Leo swindled or betrayed your partners. Now they've kidnapped my son. If I don't give them that money, there's no telling what they'll do to him."

Garcia's eyes glittered with a warning that made Willow shiver and sink back into the chair. If he didn't have the answers they needed or refused to help her, how could she save Sam?

BRETT TRIED TO get into Gus Garcia's head, but he didn't know what made the man tick. The only reason he could fathom that the man had confessed and covered for his partners was money.

But if he thought his partners had betrayed him, why wouldn't he want to help them now?

"Listen, Mr. Garcia, I don't understand why you'd cover for Howard or anyone else, but if you tell us where Leo hid the money or who's holding it, I'll write you a check myself. How does a hundred thousand sound?"

Garcia heaved a breath, sat down, looked down at his scarred hands and studied them as if he was wrestling with the decision.

When he lifted his head, his eyes were flat. "I told you I don't know where any money is. Maybe he hid it in that house he lived in at the time."

"What house?"

Garcia shrugged. "Some place in Cheyenne."

Anger shot through Brett. He would find this house, but he wanted more. "Listen to me, a little boy's life may depend on us finding that cash."

A gambit of dark emotions splintered Garcia's face. "Leo was a liar and a thief. I ain't heard from him since I was incarcerated."

Brett stood with a curse, then tossed his card at the man. "If you think of anything that can help us, call me."

Willow looked pale as the guard led Garcia out.

"What do we do now?" she asked.

"Find that damned house where Leo lived. Maybe he did hide it somewhere inside."

Frustration knotted Brett's insides, though. Finding the money there was a long shot. And they were running out of leads.

If they didn't turn up something soon, he'd contact his financial advisor to liquidate some funds. It wouldn't be the full ransom, but it might be enough to fool the men into releasing Sam.

GUS'S GUT CHURNED as the guard led him down the hall and shoved him back into his cell.

He wanted to punch something, but that guard was watching him with eagle eyes, and if he misbehaved they'd throw him in the hole. Worse, it would go on his record, and so far he'd managed to stay clean this past year.

If he messed up, he wouldn't make parole. And making parole meant everything to him.

But dammit, nothing was right.

Leo and those other two sons of bitches that he took the fall for were supposed to lay low and give him his cut when he was released.

But it sounded as if Leo had betrayed them and run off with the money.

He gritted his teeth as the cell door slammed shut. He hated that sound.

Why had he let them coerce him into lying for them?

His wife's and little girl's faces flashed in his mind and his heart felt heavy. He knew why. He'd had no choice.

They'd threatened Valeria and his kid. That was the only reason he'd helped them with the rustling operation in the first damn place.

And the woman claimed they might hurt her little boy if they didn't get what they wanted.

Indecision tormented him. McCullen had offered him enough money that he could take his family far away and live the good life, if he talked.

But if he talked, they would go after *his* family.

All he had to do was wait out one more year of his sentence, and he'd be a free man, then he'd be released and he'd protect them.

They were the only thing in the world that he had to live for.

Chapter Ten

Willow fought a sense of despair as they drove away from the prison. "Do you think Mr. Garcia is lying? Holding out for his share of that half million?"

Brett started the engine and drove through security. "I don't know. I think there's more to the story. If he thinks his partners, or Leo, are trying to cut him out, he probably would have taken the hundred thousand I offered him. That's a lot of money for an ex-con."

He was right. Which worried her even more. If Garcia didn't know where the money was, how could *they* find it?

"Do you know the address of the house where Leo lived after you separated?" Brett asked.

Willow racked her brain. "I think I can find it. A few bills came after Leo left and I forwarded them to him." She searched her phone, but she hadn't entered it in the contact information.

Frantic, she accessed her notes section and

scrolled through them. "Here it is. 389 Indian Trail Drive. It's outside Cheyenne."

"It'll take us a while to get there," Brett said. "I know you didn't sleep last night, Willow. Close your eyes and rest while I drive."

Willow looked out at the desolate countryside with the mountain ridges in the distance and the rocky barren land, and fresh tears threatened.

Where was her little boy? Was he cold or hungry? Were the men holding him taking care of him?

The storm clouds were thickening, growing darker. Sam would be getting anxious about the weather, about not coming home. He needed her.

BRETT WAITED UNTIL Willow's breathing grew steady, and she'd fallen into a sound sleep. His phone buzzed again. *Kitty. Dammit*, she was persistent.

He ignored it and phoned his financial planner and manager, Frank Cotton.

"What's up, Brett? Do you have some new investments you need handling?"

"Not exactly. I want you to see how much cash I can liquidate and how quickly."

A tense silent moment passed. "You want *cash*? May I ask the reason? Are you planning a big trip somewhere? Are you purchasing property?"

No, but he might need to sell to Maddox. Only

if he asked Maddox, his brother would want an explanation. He could approach Ray, but he doubted Ray had the money to buy him out.

"I'm not ready to discuss my plans yet," Brett said. "But it's important. And Frank, keep this matter confidential."

"Brett, don't tell me you knocked up some young girl."

Brett ground his molars. Was that what Frank thought of him? What others thought about him? "Thanks for the vote of confidence, Frank, but it's nothing like that. Just do what I ask and keep your mouth shut." Furious, he hung up.

Snippets of his past flashed back. The rodeo groupies clamoring after him after his rides. Throwing themselves at him in hotels and bars. All wanting a piece of the celebrity.

Girls with no real clear dreams of their own, except to bag a man and live off his money.

Unlike Willow, who'd built her own life and was devoted to her little boy. Shy Willow who'd stolen his heart, but hadn't made demands on him when the itch to leave Pistol Whip had called his name.

No wonder Frank thought he might have knocked up some young thing. He had left a trail of women across the states. But he didn't remember their names or faces.

Only they'd filled that empty void in his bed,

when he'd craved loving from a woman, and Willow wasn't there.

His father's praise for following his dreams echoed in his ears. He'd always thought he and his daddy were alike, that his father had regretted marrying and settling down so young. Had regretted being saddled with three boys to raise.

Brett had been determined not to make the same mistake.

But now he'd achieved success and fame, and plenty of money, but this past year he'd been restless as hell.

Lonely.

How could he have been lonely, when all he had to do was walk into a bar and he'd have a pretty woman in his bed for the night?

He glanced over at Willow, and the answer hit him swift and hard. He was lonely because none of those women were Willow.

His phone buzzed. *Maddox.*

He took a deep breath and connected the call. "Yeah?"

"What the *hell* were you looking for on my computer?"

Brett gripped the steering wheel as he veered onto the highway toward Cheyenne. "I just needed to do some research. What's the big deal?"

"The big deal is that you used my password

to access police files. Why were you looking at arrest records?"

Brett's temper flared. "You checked up on me?"

"I knew you were lying earlier, so I checked the browser history." Maddox released an angry sigh. "Now tell me what you were doing? Are you in some kind of trouble?"

First Frank, now his brother. And here, he'd considered confiding in Maddox.

"Can't you just trust me for once?" Brett snapped.

A heartbeat passed. Brett didn't know if Maddox planned to answer.

"Listen, Brett, if you are in trouble, tell me. I know we don't always see eye to eye, but I'll see what I can do to help."

Emotions twisted Brett's chest. Would Maddox put himself on the line to help him?

Maybe, but he couldn't take the chance. Not with Sam's life.

"Actually I might need you to buy me out of the ranch."

A longer silence this time, one that reeked of disappointment. "So that's it? You made a fortune out there on the circuit, but you've blown it all. What are you into, Brett? Gambling? Women?"

His words cut Brett to the bone. "I'm not into anything."

Maddox didn't seem to hear him, though. "I

knew you didn't care about Dad or me or Ray, but I thought you might have some allegiance to Horseshoe Creek."

His brother's disgusted voice tore at Brett. He *did* care about all of them. And he wanted part of that land more than he'd realized. Horseshoe Creek was his home. His roots.

Where he'd always thought he'd return once his wild days ended. Of course, like a fool, he'd thought Willow would be waiting...

Maddox heaved a breath. "How soon would you need to be bought out?"

Brett's gut churned. "As soon as possible."

Maddox cursed. "All right. I'll see what I can do. If I see Ray, I'll mention it to him, in case he wants part of your share."

Brett hated the thought of selling out to his brothers. Even more, he hated that Maddox thought he didn't give a damn about Horseshoe Creek.

But if they didn't locate the money Leo had stolen, he would sell his share in a heartbeat to save Willow's son.

WILLOW STIRRED FROM a restless sleep as Brett rolled to a stop in front of a small brick ranch house set off the road with a garage to the left and a barn out back. The house looked fairly well kept, although the barn was rotting and obviously wasn't being used for farming.

"Was Leo living here with someone else?" Brett asked.

"I don't know. It's possible."

Brett turned to her. "Were you the one who asked to get out of the marriage, Willow?"

"Yes." She reached for the doorknob. "But he didn't argue. He wanted out. That much was obvious." Doris's words echoed in her head. Leo needed a respectable wife so nobody in town would ask questions.

But respectable to *whom*? He hadn't told his father about her or Sam.

"He was the fool for not wanting to be with you," Brett murmured.

Willow swallowed hard. "You left me, too, Brett." She regretted the words the moment she said them.

Brett's eyes flickered with pain and truth of her statement.

"It doesn't matter now," Willow said. "All that matters is getting Sam back."

Brett's gaze latched with hers, and he started to say something, but she opened the door and hurried up the sidewalk. This was not the time for a personal discussion of the past.

That would come. But first she had to bring Sam home.

Brett caught up to her just as she punched the doorbell. He surveyed the property as if looking for signs of trouble. The door squeaked open, and a middle-aged woman in a nurse's uniform appeared at the door. Behind her, Willow noticed a white-haired woman in a wheelchair.

"Can I help you?" the woman asked.

"My name is Willow James, and this is Brett McCullen." Brett tipped his Stetson in greeting, and Willow forged ahead. "We'd like to talk to you, Miss…?"

"Eleanor Patterson," the woman said. "What's this about?"

Willow offered her a tentative smile. "I was married to a man named Leo Howard who lived in this house. How long have you lived here?"

"Just a few months. We needed a one-story, so we found this place."

"Did you know Mr. Howard?" Brett asked.

Eleanor angled her head toward Brett, her eyes narrowed, then lighting up in recognition. "You look familiar."

Brett's handsome face slid into one of his charming smiles. "You might recognize me from the rodeo circuit, ma'am."

She snapped her fingers. "That's where it was. My goodness, you're more handsome in person than you are in the magazines."

Irritation nagged at Willow.

"Thanks," Brett said with a smile. "Ma'am, we don't mean to bother you, but did you know Leo Howard?"

"No, the house was vacant when the Realtor showed it to me."

"Did the previous tenant leave anything here when he left?" Willow asked. "Maybe some boxes or papers."

"I really don't know." Eleanor gestured toward the older woman in the chair. "Now if you'll excuse me, it's time for her medication."

"Please think hard," Willow said. "I'm looking for some important documents that I think he put somewhere."

Eleanor looked back and forth between them, then sighed. "The house was basically empty, but now that I think about it, there were a few old boxes in the attic."

"Would you mind if we take a look?" Brett gave her another flirtatious smile, and she waved him toward the hallway where a door led to an attic. Willow followed him, uneasy at the way the woman in the wheelchair watched them, as if she thought they intended to rob her.

Dust motes drifted downward and fluttered through the attic as they climbed the steps and looked across the dark interior. Three plain brown boxes were stacked against the far wall, a ratty blanket on top.

They crossed the space to them, and Brett set the first box on the floor. Willow opened it and began to dig through it while Brett worked on the second box. Flannel shirts, jeans and a dusty pair of work boots were stuffed in the box Willow examined, along with an old pocket watch that no longer worked, and a box of cigars.

Odd. Leo hadn't smoked.

"There's a couple of fake IDs in here," Brett said. "A few letters, it looks like from Doris, but Leo never opened them."

Willow spotted another envelope in the box and removed it. Inside, she found several photographs. "Look at these." She spread them out—a picture of Leo's father, then Doris, then Gus Garcia and two other men. Were those Leo's partners?

He slid another box over between them and lifted the top. Inside lay a .38 caliber gun and some ammunition. Beside it, he found another driver's license under the name of Lamar Ranger, yet it bore Leo's photo.

Oddly another pair of boots sat inside. Curious, Brett searched inside the boot but found nothing. Still wondering why the boots were stowed with the gun instead of the other box of clothes, he flipped the boots over and noticed one of the soles was loose.

"What is it?" Willow asked.

Brett removed his pocketknife and ripped the sole of the shoe off and found a folded piece of paper inside. He opened it and spread it on the floor, his heart thundering.

"A map."

Willow leaned closer to examine it. "You think this map will lead us to the place where Leo stashed the money?"

"That's exactly what I'm thinking." He folded it and put it in his pocket, then set the gun and fake ID in one box to take with them. They might need them for evidence.

Willow brushed dust from her jeans as they descended the steps and shut the attic.

Eleanor appeared in the hallway, her brows furrowed. "Did you find what you were looking for?"

"Not really," Brett said. "But we're taking this one with us. The boots are special to Willow."

Willow thanked her, then she and Brett hurried outside to his truck. She hoped Brett was right. If that map led them to the money, she could trade it for Sam and bring him back home where he belonged.

BRETT'S PULSE HAMMERED as he drove away from Eleanor's. He waited until they'd reached the dirt road he'd seen on the map, then pulled over, unfolded it and studied it.

"Where is it?" Willow asked.

Brett pointed to the crude notations on the map. Symbols of trees and rocks in various formations that must be significant, signs that would lead the way to his hiding spot.

"If it's there, and we find it," Willow said, "maybe we can end this tonight."

Brett gave a quick nod, although he was still worried that the kidnapper would hurt Sam.

He fired up the engine again, and turned onto the dirt road while Willow pointed out the landmarks.

"There's the rock in the shape of a turtle." A hundred feet down the road. "Those bushes, they form a ring." Another mile. "There's the creek."

He made each turn, the distance growing closer until he spotted the ridge with water dripping over it creating a small waterfall. Willow tapped the map. "Hopefully it's in this spot, hidden under the falls."

Brett pulled over and parked, then got out. The shovels they'd used to bury Leo were still in the back, so he retrieved them and carried them along the trail to the ridge overhang.

Willow knelt and they both examined the wall of rock. She pointed to an etching of a star. "I think the money may be buried here."

Brett propped one shovel by the rock and began to dig. Willow yanked her hair back into a ponytail, and jammed the second shovel into the dirt.

For several minutes they worked, digging deeper, but suddenly a gunshot sounded and pinged off the rock beside him.

Brett threw an arm around Willow and pushed her down, just as a second bullet whizzed by their heads.

Chapter Eleven

"Who's shooting at us?" Willow cried.

"I don't know, but the shot is coming from behind that boulder." Brett gestured toward the bushes beside the falls. "Run behind those bushes."

Willow remained hunkered down, but crept toward the left by the brush. Another shot pinged off the rocks at their feet, and he grabbed her hand and dragged her from the ledge behind some rocks.

"Stay down, Willow."

"What are you going to do?"

"Find out who the hell is firing at us."

Willow grabbed his arm to hold him back. "Please don't go, Brett. I don't want you to get hurt."

"I'm not going to wait here like a sitting duck." Brett ushered her down to the ground, then grabbed his shovel and circled back behind more bushes and trees so he could sneak up on the shooter.

Rocks skittered and a man scrambled down a path. Brett chased after him, but the man veered to the right and cut through a patch of brush to a black sedan parked behind a boulder.

Brett looked back and motioned for Willow to meet him at the car. She took off running, and he jogged down the path, trying to catch up with the shooter. By the time they reached the truck, the sedan roared away.

Brett tossed the shovel into the back of the truck, grabbed his rifle and started the engine. Willow jumped inside, looking shaken. He hit the accelerator and sped behind the sedan, determined to catch him.

"Can you see the tag number?"

Willow leaned forward and squinted as the driver spun onto a side dirt road. "SJ3...I can't see the rest."

The truck bounced over ruts in the road, spitting dust and gravel as he closed the distance. Tires squealed and the driver sped up, trees and brush flying past as he maneuvered a turn. A tire blew and the car swerved. The driver tried to regain control, but he overcompensated and the car spun in a circle, then careened toward a thicket of trees.

The passenger side slammed into the massive trunk, glass shattering and spraying the air and ground.

Brett grabbed his rifle as he slowed to a stop, and motioned for Willow to stay inside the truck.

"Be careful, Brett. He tried to kill us."

He certainly had, and Brett aimed to find out the reason. And if the bastard had Sam, he'd shove this rifle down his throat.

He raised the gun in front of him, scrutinizing the car as he inched forward. The passenger side was crunched, but the driver's side was intact. Still, the front windshield had shattered, and he didn't see movement inside.

Instincts as alert as they were when he climbed on a bull, he crept closer, his eyes trained on the driver. Daylight was waning, the sun sinking behind clouds that threatened rain, the temperature dropping.

He kept the gun aimed as he carefully opened the car door. It screeched, but opened enough for him to see that the driver was alive. Blood dotted his forehead where he'd hit his head.

Brett jammed the gun to the man's temple, then snagged him by the shirt collar so he could see his face. White, about forty years old, scruffy face, scar above his right eye.

"Who the hell are you?" Brett asked.

The man groaned and tried to open his eyes. He wiped at the blood with the back of his hand.

Brett jammed the tip of the rifle harder against his skull, and the man stiffened.

"Don't shoot, buddy. Please don't kill me."

"You tried to kill me and the woman I was with." Anger hardened his tone. "I want to know the reason."

"I wasn't going to kill you," the man said, his voice cracking. "I just wanted to scare you off."

Brett clenched his jaw but kept the gun at the man's head. "Why?"

"Because Eleanor called and said she thought you knew where the money was."

So Eleanor had lied. "Was she working with Leo or *sleeping* with him?" Brett asked.

"Neither, I'm Eleanor's husband, Ralph," the man said. "She takes care of Leo's grandmother. Leo stayed with her for a while, then moved out."

"Where did he move?"

"I don't know. He told Eleanor he'd pay her to be the old lady's nurse, but then he left her high and dry, and me and Eleanor have been trying to pay the bills."

"I thought she said she didn't know Leo."

"She didn't. They set it up over the phone."

Unfortunately he believed the man. Leo had been scum through and through.

The man fidgeted. "Did you find the money?"

"You know about the money?" Brett asked.

"Leo's grandmother told us he had a big bagful. She wanted it to help us. And Leo owes us—"

"We haven't found any cash," Brett said. "And before you ask, I was not working with Leo. He's a dirt bag who *stole* that money. He married the woman you were shooting at and lied to her, then he turned up dead. The people he betrayed kidnapped her son."

The man's eyes widened in shock. "Leo's dead."

"Yeah and if I don't find that money, that little boy may be, too." Brett gripped him tighter. "Do you know where he is?"

The man shook his head back and forth, his eyes panicked. "No, I like kids. I'd never do anything to hurt one."

"What about the men Leo was in cahoots with? Did you know them?"

"No, I swear. When Leo called Eleanor to hire her, she said he seemed nervous. But she likes geriatric patients and wanted to help the old woman."

"She didn't mention a name, or maybe a place Leo said he was going when he left that house? Maybe another address?"

He shook his head again. "If he had, I would have paid him a visit myself. When you showed up, we thought you might lead us back to him."

Brett released the man with a silent curse.

He turned and walked back toward Willow, hating that he had no answers yet.

WILLOW COULDN'T BELIEVE her eyes. Brett was letting the man who'd tried to kill them go.

"Who was he?" Willow asked as soon as he returned to the truck. "Why was he shooting at us?"

"Eleanor's husband. The woman in the wheelchair was Leo's grandmother. He hired Eleanor as a caretaker, but ran off without paying her."

"He really was awful," Willow said, her heart going out to the elderly woman.

"Apparently Eleanor and her husband were desperate financially. They thought you and I knew where Leo was, or at least where his money was, so he followed us. He wasn't trying to kill us, just scare us off so he could take the cash."

"So Leo wrecked that couple's lives, just like he did mine." Willow grimaced. Of course it was her fault for trusting him, for allowing him to be around Sam.

Brett started the truck and drove back toward the falls. When he parked this time, he managed to get closer to the area where they were digging. He carefully scanned for anyone else who might have followed.

"You can stay in the truck, Willow. I have to see if the money is there."

"No, I'm going with you."

Again, they grabbed the shovels and strode to the ridge, then ducked below the falls. The hole they'd started was still there, so he jammed the shovel in and continued to dig for the money.

Minutes ticked by, the wind picking up as rain began to fall, slashing them with the cold moisture. By the time he'd dug a few feet, the shovel hit rock. "It's not here."

"It has to be," Willow said, desperate.

Brett wiped his forehead with the back of his sleeve. "Let me try a different spot."

They spent the next hour digging around the original location, but again and again, hit stone.

Finally Willow leaned against a boulder. "If he put it here, someone must have already found it."

"Or he moved it," Brett said.

Willow shivered from the cold and the ugly truth. Another night was setting in.

Another night she'd have to wonder where her little boy was and if she'd ever see him again.

THEY MADE THE DRIVE back to Horseshoe Creek in silence. Brett hated the strain on Willow's face, but he understood her fear because he felt it in his bones.

He'd been certain that map would lead them to the money.

But Leo could have already retrieved the cash and moved it. Only where had he put it?

Maddox's truck was parked at the main house, so Brett bypassed it and drove straight to the cabin. "Was there any place that was significant to Leo? A place he liked to go riding?"

Willow rubbed her forehead. "Not that I know of."

"How about a place he took you and Sam?"

She looked out the window, as if she was lost in thought. "Honestly, Brett, Leo never spent much time with Sam."

He gritted his teeth. The poor kid. He needed a father. And it sounded like Leo hadn't been one at all.

Brett thought about his own father and how much he missed him now. They'd clashed over the years, but even when Joe McCullen was hard on him, Brett had known it was because his old man cared about him. That he was trying to raise him to be a decent man.

They walked up to the cabin together, and he unlocked the door. He ached for his father, for Willow and for her son, who was probably scared right now and wanted his mother.

"I'm sorry he let you down, Willow." He turned to her, his heart in his throat. "I'm sorry I let you down, too."

Willow's face crumpled, and tears trickled down her eyes. "Brett, what if—"

"Shh." He pulled her into his arms and stroked her hair. "Don't think like that. These guys want that money. If we don't find the cash Leo stole,

I'll pay. I already called my financial manager and he's working on liquidating some funds."

Willow looked up at him with such fear and tenderness that he knew he'd do anything in the world to make it right for her. Then she lifted her hand to his cheek, and he couldn't resist.

He dipped his head and closed his mouth over hers.

Overwhelmed with affection for her, he cradled her gently, and deepened the kiss, telling her with his mouth how much he cared for her. How much he'd missed her.

How much he wanted to alleviate her pain.

Willow leaned into him and ran her hands up his back, clinging to him just as she once had when they were friends and lovers. Regret for the years he'd missed with her swelled inside him.

He stroked her hair, then dropped kisses into it, then down her ear and neck and throat. She rubbed his calf with her foot, stoking his desire, and he cupped her hips and pressed her closer to him.

Need and hunger ignited between them, and their kisses turned frenzied and more passionate. He inched her backward toward the sofa.

But his phone buzzed, and they pulled apart. Their ragged breathing punctuated the air as he checked the caller ID. *Unknown.*

He punched Connect. "Brett McCullen."

A second passed.

"Hello?"

"Mr. McCullen, you talked to my husband, Gus, today at the prison."

Brett straightened. "Yes. I was hoping he could help me. Did he give you my number?"

"Yes, although he didn't want me to call. But he explained to me about the little boy. I'm… sorry."

Brett frowned.

"I…think I might be able to help."

"You can help? *How?*"

"I can't discuss this over the phone. Can you meet me?"

"Of course. Just tell me the place."

"The Wagon Wheel. An hour."

The Wagon Wheel was a restaurant/bar near Laramie. "I'll be there."

Chapter Twelve

"Who was that?" Willow asked when Brett pocketed his phone and reached for his hat.

"Gus Garcia's wife. She wants to meet me tonight."

Willow's heart jumped to her throat. "She knows where Sam is."

Brett grabbed his keys. "She didn't say. But if she has any information that might lead to that money, I need to go."

Willow reached for her jacket, but Brett placed his hand on her arm.

"I can handle this if you want to stay here and rest."

Willow shook her head. "No way. Besides, if this woman holds back, maybe I can appeal to her on a woman-to-woman basis."

Brett's mouth twitched slightly. "I can't argue with that."

The wind splattered them with light raindrops as they ran to his truck. As Brett drove toward

The Wagon Wheel, silence fell between them, thick with fear for Sam. Still, Willow couldn't help but remember the kiss they'd shared. A hot, passionate, hungry kiss that only made her crave another.

And reminded her how much she'd loved Brett.

And how painful it had been when he'd left her years ago.

She couldn't allow herself to hope that they could rekindle that love. And when Brett discovered Sam was his…

She'd face that when they got her little boy back.

It took half an hour to reach The Wagon Wheel, a bar/restaurant that specialized in barbecue and beer. Pickups, SUVs and a couple of motorcycles filled the parking lot, the wooden wheel lit up against the darkness.

Willow pulled her scarf over her head as they hurried to the door. Country music blared from the inside as they entered. The place was rustic with deer and elk heads, saddles, saddle blankets and other ranch tools on the walls. Wood floors, pine benches and tables, and checkered table-cloths gave it a cozy country feel.

Willow dug her hands in her jacket pockets. "How do we recognize her?"

Brett shrugged, but his phone buzzed with a text. When he looked down, the message said, Back booth on the right.

"That way." Brett led Willow to the rear of the restaurant where a small Hispanic woman with big dark eyes sat with her hands knotted on the table.

"Mrs. Garcia?"

She nodded, her gaze darting over Willow, then she looked back down at her hands as if wrestling with whether or not to flee.

Willow covered the woman's hand with her own and they slid into the booth. "I appreciate you meeting us. My name is Willow. Tell me your name."

"Valeria," the woman said in a low voice. "I… my husband will be upset that I come."

Willow squeezed her hand. "I don't want to cause you trouble, but my son is missing, Valeria, and I need help."

Valeria gave them both a wary look. "You don't understand. My husband…he not talk because he scared for me and little Ana Sofia."

Willow's heart pounded. "Ana Sofia?"

"Our little girl. She's eight." Valeria pulled a photo from her handwoven purse and showed it to them. "She…is so sweet and so tiny. And Gus went to prison so those bad men wouldn't kill us."

Willow tensed. "Someone threatened your little girl?"

Valeria nodded and curled her fingers into Willow's. But she looked directly at Brett, her eyes pleading, "If I talk to you, you take us some place where they can't hurt us?"

Brett spoke through clenched teeth. "Yes, ma'am. I promise. I'll pay for protection for you myself."

BRETT HAD NO patience for any man who would hurt a woman. "Who threatened you and your daughter, Valeria?"

"If I tell you, they may hurt my Gus."

"He's in prison," Willow said.

Brett understood Mrs. Garcia's fear, though. If someone wanted to get to Gus, they could.

"No one will know about this conversation," Brett assured her.

"Just tell us what happened," Willow said softly.

Valeria pulled her hand from Willow's and twisted them together in her lap. "*Sí.* I do this for the little boy, miss. I cannot stand for anyone to hurt children."

"Neither can I," Willow said, a look of motherly understanding passing between the two women.

"You see, Gus, he work for this rancher named Boyle Gates. Mr. Gates have big spread, but some say he cheat and steal so he be biggest, wealthiest rancher in Wyoming."

"What exactly did Gus do for Gates?" Brett asked.

"He was ranch hand," Valeria said. "Gus proud man. He work hard. But one day Mr. Gates accuse him of stealing money from his safe in house.

My Gus not do it, but man named Dale Franklin say he saw Gus take it."

"Dale Franklin? He died, didn't he?"

"Yes." Her voice quivered. "Gus think they kill him. He was working with a rustling cattle ring. They tell Gus they do same to him and us if he not help them."

"What exactly did they want him to do?" Brett asked.

She dabbed at her eyes with a colorful handkerchief. "Steal cattle." Her lip quivered. "Gus not want to, but they say they fix things with Mr. Gates so he keep job and they pay him, too. He still say no, but then they talk about hurting me and our Ana Sofia, he go along."

"And when the men were caught, Gus took the fall to protect you."

She nodded, her eyes blurring with tears. "Gus try to be good in prison so he get out one day. That reason he not talk to you."

"You said *they*, but you only mentioned a man named Dale Franklin. Who else was involved?" Willow asked.

Valeria looked nervous again, but Brett assured her once more that he would protect her and her child. "I'll also do whatever I can to help Gus get paroled. Just give me the men's names."

Valerie heaved a big breath. "Jasper Day and Wally Norman."

"Do they still work for Mr. Gates?" Brett asked.

She shrugged. "I think Mr. Norman, he wind up in prison, too. Not sure he still there."

"Valeria, whoever is holding Sam believes Leo Howard had that money and stashed it somewhere. Do you or Gus know where he would have hidden it?"

She shook her head no. "Mr. Howard was leader. Gus said he was brains."

Brains without a conscience.

Brett wished the bastard was still alive so he could beat the hell out of him. Because of him, Willow's little boy was in danger.

"Valeria, where is your little girl now?"

"At Miss Vera's. I clean her house."

"Let us follow you and pick up Ana Sofia. There's an extra cabin on my family's ranch where the two of you can stay. You'll be safe there."

Willow took Valeria's hands in hers. "I promise, no one will look for you at Horseshoe Creek."

Brett's gut tightened. He should discuss this with Maddox first, but Horseshoe Creek was as much his land as it was his brother's.

That is, until he sold his share to Maddox. Then he would have no stake in the land. No ties to it himself.

Was that what he wanted?

No, but he'd do it for Sam.

WILLOW FOLLOWED VALERIA inside the small shack where Valeria lived. Ever since her husband had been incarcerated, the poor woman had been cleaning Ms. Vera's house, as well as rooms at a motel to put food on the table.

Willow didn't condone Mr. Garcia's illegal activities, but if he'd been coerced to help the other men out of fear, she could understand. Just look at the lengths she had gone to in the past couple of days for her own son.

Little Ana Sofia was a tiny dark-haired girl with waist-length black braids and the biggest brown eyes Willow had ever seen. She clung to her mother's skirt as Valeria explained that they were taking a trip for a few days.

The child's questioning look only compounded the turmoil raging inside Willow.

How could she ever have married a man who would threaten a family like Leo had?

Had she been that desperate for a father for her baby?

No...she'd been desperate to forget Brett. She'd seen the tabloids of the women throwing themselves at him and had needed comfort. And Leo had stroked her ego—at first.

All part of his ruse to cover up the fact that he was a criminal.

"This is Miss Willow," Valeria said. "She and Mr. Brett are going to let us stay on their ranch."

Not *her* ranch. Brett's and his brothers'. But

Willow didn't comment. At one time she'd fantasized about marrying Brett and the two of them carving out a home on a piece of the McCullen land.

But that dream had died years ago.

"Hi, Ana, you have beautiful hair." Willow stroked one of her braids. "And beautiful big eyes."

"They're like my daddy's." Ana's lower lip quivered. "But I don't get to see him anymore."

Valeria looked stricken, but Willow patted the little girl's back. "Well, maybe one day soon, you will. And you can tell him all about the horses and cows you see on Mr. Brett's ranch. Would you like that?"

"I like horses," the little girl said.

Valeria hugged Willow. "Thank you, Miss Willow."

Willow's throat closed. "No, Valeria, thank you."

Because of Valeria's courage, they might have a lead on how to find the money Willow needed.

WILLOW HELPED VALERIA and her daughter settle into a cabin near the one where Brett and Willow were staying. The sound of an engine made him step outside the cabin, and he cursed.

Maddox in his police SUV. What was he doing here?

Wind battered the trees and sent a few twigs

and limbs down, a light rain adding to the cold dreariness as evening set in.

Brett jammed his hands in his pockets and waited, contemplating an explanation as Maddox parked and strode up to the porch. Rain dripped from his cowboy hat and jacket as he ducked under the roof.

"What's going on, Brett?"

Brett tensed at his brother's gruff tone. Maddox had a way of saying things that reeked of disapproval even without using specific words.

"I decided to stay in that cabin over there. And a friend of mine needed a place, so she's staying here."

Maddox arched a brow. "A woman? She's not staying with *you*?"

Brett swallowed back a biting retort. He'd be damned if he'd admit that Willow was staying with him. "No, she just needs a safe place for her and her little girl for a few days."

Maddox crossed his arms. "Brett, is this woman one of your conquests?" He lowered his voice. "Is the kid *yours*?"

Anger slashed through Brett. "You *would* think the worst of me, wouldn't you?" He squared his shoulders, making him eye to eye with Maddox. "I wouldn't do that to a woman. And if the child *was* mine, I'd take responsibility."

Animosity bubbled between them, born of years apart—and the years they'd fought as kids.

"I'm sorry," Maddox said quietly. "I guess I jumped to conclusions."

Brett released a tense breath. Maddox didn't apologize often.

"She's in trouble," Brett said in a low voice. "Can't you just trust me for once, Maddox, and let her stay here without asking questions?"

Maddox studied him for another full minute, then gave a clipped nod. "Okay, little brother. Do you want me to have my deputy or one of the ranch hands drive by and check on them tonight?"

Brett shrugged. "Maybe one of the ranch hands. I don't think the deputy needs to come." Sweat beaded on his brow. What if the deputy drove around and found Leo's grave?

"Okay, I'll tell Ron to swing by."

"Thanks, Maddox."

Maddox made a clicking sound with his teeth. "I guess it's time we both start trusting each other, right?"

"Right." Brett's gut knotted with guilt as Maddox strode back to his SUV. Maddox would kick his butt when he learned what Brett had done.

It would also destroy any chance of a reconciliation between him and his brother.

WILLOW BATTLED TEARS as she listened to Brett's conversation with Maddox. Brett wouldn't have abandoned a child.

She should tell him about Sam.

After all, he was putting his relationship with his brother on the line for her. She owed him the truth. But he cut her off before she could speak.

"I'm going to see that rancher tonight. Stay here with Valeria."

Willow glanced down at her phone, willing it to ring. But the picture of little Sam that the kidnapper had sent stared back.

She wrapped her coat around her. "No, I'm going with you. I want to see his reaction to the picture of my son."

Sam pushed aside the grilled cheese the man set in front of him. "I want my mommy."

"Well, your mommy's not here, kid. Now eat the sandwich."

Sam picked at the burnt edge, then set the plate on the floor "It's black. And it gots the crust on it and Mommy cuts the crust off."

The man's pudgy face puffed up like a big fat pig's. Then he picked up the sandwich and shoved it toward Sam's mouth.

Sam's stomach growled, but he hated the man, and he wasn't going to eat the nasty thing so he turned his head away.

The mean man probably put roaches in the sandwiches or spiders or maybe he even spit tobacco in it. He'd seen him spitting that brown stuff in that can.

"Fine, you little brat. Starve." He hurled the

sandwich at the wall. It hit, then fell to the floor, a mangled mess.

Sam fought tears. "When are you gonna take me back?"

The man glared at him, then slammed the door. Sam heard the key turning and threw himself at the door, beating on it. "I wanna go home! Let me go!"

He beat and beat until his fists hurt, and snot bubbled in his nose.

Don't be a baby, he told himself. *Cowboys don't cry.*

He wiped his nose on his sleeve and looked around the dingy room. He needed to find a way out, but those windows were nailed shut.

He hunted for something sharp to use to stab the man with if he came back. A knife or a nail or a pair of scissors. But he couldn't find anything but a broken plastic comb.

The rope they'd first tied his hands with was on the floor. It wasn't long enough to make a lasso like the cowboys used.

He wound the rope around his fingers and tried to remember the knots he'd seen in that book he sneaked from the library. It had pictures of roping calves and horseback riding and trick riding.

His mama had another book in the table by her bed, too. She pretended she didn't like rodeos, but he'd seen her looking at pictures of that famous rodeo star. Only those pictures made her cry.

He laid the rope in his lap and twisted and turned it, then tried again and again. If he could trip that mean man, and tie him up like a calf, he could run and run till he found his mommy again.

Chapter Thirteen

Brett waited until the rancher showed up to guard Valeria and her daughter.

"Is she running from a husband?" Ron asked.

Brett shrugged, not wanting to explain. "Something like that."

"I'll make sure no one bothers her tonight."

"Thanks." Brett shook the man's hand. One thing he could always count on was that Maddox hired good men.

He met Willow at the truck. His phone buzzed again as he drove toward Gates's ranch. *Kitty.* He ignored the call.

Why couldn't she take the hint? A second later, his phone rang again.

"Aren't you going to answer that, Brett?"

"No, it's no one important."

Willow's brows lifted. "It's your girlfriend, isn't it?"

Brett's pulse clamored. He didn't want to discuss the women in his past with Willow. "I don't have a girlfriend."

Willow released a sardonic laugh. "Oh, that's right. You have a different woman in every city."

He hated that she was right. "Where did you get that idea?"

"Pictures of you and your lovers are plastered all over the rodeo magazines. How could I *not* know? Let's see. There was Bethany in Laredo, Aurora in Austin, then Carly in Houston, Pauline in El Paso—"

Brett held up a hand. "Okay, so I've dated a few women. *You* got married." And had a child with another man. And within a year after his last visit home. A visit that had made him think they might have a future.

But she'd squashed that with her wedding.

"You're right. I guess we both moved on."

Had they? Or had he just been biding time, hoping one day to reconcile with Willow?

The rain fell harder, slashing the windshield and roof, forcing him to drive slower through the rocky terrain.

"By the way, congratulations on all your success, Brett." Willow looked out the window as she spoke. "You followed your dreams and became exactly what you always wanted to be."

Brett gripped the steering wheel as he sped around a curve and headed down the long road toward Gates's spread, the Circle T. Willow's words taunted him.

He had achieved success on the circuit. And he didn't have to go without a woman. There were plenty of groupies out there. But they wanted the same thing—the fame, the money, the cameras…

All carbon copies. *Shallow.*

None of them wanted the real Brett or cared to know about his family. Or that sometimes he regretted leaving Pistol Whip and the chasm between him and his brothers. That when his mother died, he'd fallen apart and missed her so much that he'd cried himself to sleep every night.

That he wanted to be as perfect as Maddox, but he hadn't been, so he'd joked his way through life. That the only thing he'd been good at was riding.

He'd certainly screwed up with Willow.

Willow gestured toward the turnoff for the ranch. "There's the sign for the Circle T."

He'd read about Gates's operation. He owned thousands of acres, raised crops and had made a name for himself in the cattle business.

At one time, Brett's father had wanted to make Horseshoe Creek just as big. He'd wanted him and Ray to help Maddox—with the three of them working together, it might have been possible.

But Brett had needed to stretch his wings. And Ray…he'd had too much anger in him. He couldn't get along with Joe or Maddox.

Willow grew more tense as they approached

the house, and kept running her finger over the photo of Sam that the kidnapper had texted.

Brett put thoughts of Horseshoe Creek and his own problems behind. He could live with Maddox hating him when this was over.

As long as he put Sam back in Willow's arms.

EVEN THOUGH IT was dark and raining, Willow could see that the Circle T spanned for miles and miles. She'd heard about the big operation and that Gates was a formidable man.

Had he earned his money and success by being involved with crooks like Leo?

She tugged her jacket hood over her head, ducking against the wind and rain as she and Brett made their way to the front door. A chunky woman in a maid's uniform answered the door and escorted them to a huge paneled office with a large cherry desk, and corner bar. Dozens of awards for Gates's quality beef cattle adorned the wall.

The maid offered them coffee, but she and Brett both declined. Her stomach was too tied in knots to think about drinking or eating anything.

A big man, she guessed around six-one, two hundred and eighty pounds, sauntered in wearing a dress Western shirt and jeans that looked as if they'd been pressed. An expensive diamond-crusted ring glittered from one hand, while a gold rope chain circled his thick neck.

Brett introduced them and shook the man's hand. Gates removed his hat and set it on his desk in a polite gesture as he greeted Willow.

Gates pulled a hand down his chin. "McCullen, you're one of Joe's boys, the one that's the big rodeo star, aren't you?"

"Yes, sir."

"I was sorry to hear about your daddy," Gates said. "He was a good man."

"Yes, he was." Brett's expression looked pained. He obviously hadn't expected condolences from the man.

"Care for a drink?" Gates gestured toward the bar, but Brett and Willow declined.

"So what do I owe the honor? You here to find out my trade secrets?" Gates emitted a blustery laugh.

Brett laughed, too, but it sounded forced. "No, sir, although if you want to share, I'm sure my brother Maddox would love to talk."

Gates harrumphed. "I guess he would."

Willow squared her shoulders. "Mr. Gates, did you know my husband, Leo Howard?"

Gates's mustache twitched with a frown as he claimed a seat behind his desk. "Name don't ring a bell."

"How about Gus Garcia?" Brett asked.

Gates's chair creaked as he leaned back in it. "That bastard tried to steal from under me. Why are you asking about him?"

"We believe that the men Garcia partnered with were in cahoots with Leo Howard."

Willow watched for a reaction, but the man didn't show one. "I don't understand. Garcia confessed and is in prison. I don't know about any partners. But since they locked Garcia up, I haven't had any more trouble."

"You knew a man named Dale Franklin was killed during the arrest? Two other men, Jasper Day and Wally Norman were also involved."

Gates planted both hands on the desk. "All I know is that after they put Garcia away, I cleaned house around here, brought in a whole new crew of hands."

He'd cleaned house to protect his business from corruption? Or to eliminate suspicion from himself for illegal activities?

Brett leaned forward, hands folded. "Do you know where we could find Day or Norman?"

"No, and I don't want to know."

Willow stood and approached his desk. "Mr. Gates, I think my ex-husband and those men rustled cattle and made a lot of money doing it, that they stashed the money somewhere, and I need to know where it is."

Gates shot up from his seat, his jowls puffing out with rage. "What the *hell*? You think I had something to do with them? Listen here, woman, they stole *from* me, not *for* me."

"Mr. Gates," Brett said, holding out a calming hand. "We aren't accusing you of anything. We just want to know if you have any idea where either of those men are."

"No." Gates started around his desk. "Now you two have worn out your welcome."

Willow flipped her phone around and jammed it in the man's face. "Look, Mr. Gates, someone kidnapped my little boy. His name is Sam. I think Day and Norman are responsible. They're demanding the money Leo made off the cattle rustling in exchange for my son. If I don't find it, I might not see my son again."

BRETT STUDIED GATES for telltale signs that he was behind the kidnapping. Gates was a formidable man. If Leo had stolen from him, he had motive for murder.

But Gates paled as he studied the photograph. "You think those men sent that to you?"

"The man didn't identify himself," Willow said. "But he said he wanted the money Leo stole. And if I don't find it, they'll hurt my little boy."

Gates pinched the bridge of his nose. "I'm sorry about your child, miss, but I don't know anything about a kidnapping or any money. And that's the gospel."

"Are you sure?" Brett asked. "You've built an empire awfully quickly. Maybe we should have your herd checked to make sure some of your cattle weren't stolen?"

Gates whirled on Brett in a rage. "How dare you come to my house and suggest such a thing. Now, get out."

"Mr. Gates," Willow cried. "If you have any idea how to find my son, please help me."

Gates's tone rumbled out, barely controlled. "I told you, I don't know anything."

Brett crossed his arms. "Think about it, Gates. Kidnapping is a capital offense. If you help—"

Gates stepped forward and jerked Brett by the arm. "I said get out."

WILLOW WAS TREMBLING as she and Brett left the Circle T.

"Do you think he was lying about knowing Leo?"

Brett's brows were furrowed as he drove away. "I think he's a ruthless man who's made a lot of money fast."

"What are we going to do now?" Willow asked. Her hopes were quickly deflating.

"I've been trying to think of another place where Leo might hide the money. You said his mother died. Where is she buried?"

Willow wrung her hands together. "I don't know. He didn't like to talk about her."

The windshield wipers swished back and forth as the rain fell, the night growing longer as she imagined little Sam locked in some scary place alone.

Brett punched in a number on his phone. "Mr. Howard, this is Brett McCullen again. Can you tell me where your wife was buried?" A pause. "Thank you."

He ended the call and spun around in the opposite direction. "She's in a memorial garden not far from Laramie."

Willow closed her eyes as he drove, but rest didn't come. Images of Sam flashed through her mind like a movie trailer. Sam being born, that little cleft chin and dimple so similar to Brett's that it had robbed her breath.

Sam, the day he'd taken his first step—they had been outside in the grass and he'd seen a butterfly and wanted to chase it. A smile curved her mouth as she remembered his squeal of delight when he'd tumbled down the hill and the butterfly had landed on his nose.

Then Christmas when he'd wanted a horseshoe set. And his third birthday when she'd taken him to the county fair, and he'd had his first pony ride. Dressed in a cowboy shirt, jeans and hat, he'd looked like a pro sitting astride the pony.

He would have loved to watch Brett at the rodeo.

But she'd known watching Brett compete would be difficult.

Every time she'd seen a tabloid with his photograph or a picture of a woman on his arm or kissing him, she'd cried. So she'd finally avoided the rodeo magazines.

Although how could she escape Brett when each time she looked at Sam, she saw his father's face?

Exhausted, she must have dozed off because when she stirred, they'd reached the graveyard. Rain and the cold made the rows of granite markers and tombstones look even more desolate.

Brett parked and reached for the door handle, but she caught his arm. "You aren't going to disturb that poor woman's grave, are you?"

A dark look crossed Brett's face. "We put Leo in the ground, Willow. I'll do whatever I have to in order to save Sam."

Tears blurred her eyes. She thought she'd loved Brett before, but even if he walked away when she got Sam back, she would always love him for what he'd done to help her.

"What the *hell* have you done?"

He clenched the phone, his knuckles white. "I did what I had to do."

"You kidnapped a kid? What were you thinking?"

"I was thinking about getting that damn money. Howard refused to tell me where he hid it."

"So you killed him?"

"He came at me and tried to grab the gun from me. It just went off."

"This is some screwed-up mess. I don't want to go to prison for kidnapping."

"What about me? I could be charged with murder." His breath quickened. "That's the reason I took the kid. I need that money to skip the country. And I figured Howard must have told his wife where it was."

"But she claims she doesn't know. She's hooked up with one of those McCullen boys and they're asking questions all over the place."

"The woman has to be lying. Let her sweat a little over the kid and she'll give it up."

Chapter Fourteen

Brett felt as if the walls were closing in. Like the fear that chewed at his gut before he rode a bull these days. The fear that he might not come out whole... Or even alive.

But he didn't care if he died, if Willow got her son back.

Still, he was playing a dangerous game. Burying dead bodies, hiding the truth from the law, desecrating a grave when he'd been taught all his life to respect the dead.

Surely Leo wouldn't have dug deep enough to disturb his mother's coffin, and he would have needed equipment if he actually stored the cash inside the casket. So it made sense that he would have dug a shallow hole.

The rain splattering the grave marker reminded him of Willow's tears and the fact that they'd just buried his father, and his tombstone hadn't been ready at the funeral. Maddox had ordered it.

He wondered what Maddox had written on the headstone.

Pushing his own grief aside, he examined the dirt on Mrs. Howard's grave, looking for signs that it had been disturbed lately. Of course, Leo could have buried the money here when he'd first married Willow.

Then he'd sat back biding his time until interest in the cattle rustling case died down and no one was looking for him.

Rain dripped off his Stetson and down into his shirt collar as he dug deeper, raking the dirt aside. Another shovelful of dirt, and he moved slightly to the right to check that area. The wet dirt was packed, but he dumped it aside, only to find more dirt.

Questions about Leo pummeled him as he continued to explore one spot then the next. Could Leo have hidden the money in Willow's house? No…she said she'd rented that place after they'd separated…

But he had gone back to see her the day he'd died…

Irritated that he had no answers, he kept digging, but forty-five minutes later, he realized his efforts were futile.

Leo had not buried the money in his mother's grave. Maybe he had some kind of moral compass after all.

Whispering an apology to the woman in the

ground, he covered the grave with the dirt again, making quick work of the mess he'd made, then smoothing it out to show some respect.

Finally satisfied that he hadn't totally desecrated the memory of the woman in the ground, he wiped rain from his face and strode back to the truck. Willow sat looking out the window over the graveyard, her eyes a mixture of hope and grief.

He wanted to make her smile again. Fill her mind with dreams and promises of a happy future, the way they'd once done when they sneaked out to the barn and made love.

"It wasn't there, was it?" she said, her voice low. Pained. Defeated.

"I'm sorry." He climbed in and reached for her, but she turned toward the window, arms wrapped around her waist, shutting down.

That frightened him more than anything. If they didn't find Sam tonight, it would be the second night she'd been without her son. The second terrifying night of wondering if he was dead or alive.

WILLOW WAITED IN the truck as Brett stopped by the cabin to check on Valeria and Ana Sofia.

When he returned to the truck, he waved to the rancher Maddox had asked to watch the woman and her child. Ron had parked himself outside the cabin and seemed to be taking his role of bodyguard seriously.

"I'm glad she's safe. She was a brave lady to help me," Willow said, her heart in her throat.

Brett drove to the cabin where they were staying. "Don't give up, Willow. I'm still working on liquidating some funds. At least enough to make a trade and satisfy these men."

She murmured her appreciation, although hope waned with every passing hour.

Brett tossed her an umbrella and she ran through the sludge up to the cabin door. As soon as they entered, she ducked into the bathroom and closed the door. Tears overflowed, her sobs so painful, she couldn't breathe.

She flipped on the shower water, undressed, climbed in and let the hot water sluice over her, mingling with her tears. When the water finally cooled, she forced herself to regain control, dried off and dragged on a big terry-cloth robe. She towel dried her hair, letting the long strands dangle around her face, took a deep breath and stepped into the den.

Brett was standing with a drink in his hand, his eyes worried as he offered her the tumbler. "Drink this. I need to clean up."

She hadn't noticed how muddy and soaked he was, but he'd been out in the freezing rain digging for that money for over an hour. He had to be cold and exhausted.

But he still looked as handsome as sin.

She accepted the shot of whiskey and carried it to the sofa where he'd lit a fire. Tired and terrified, she sank onto the couch and sipped the amber liquid, grateful for the warmth of the fire and the alcohol that burned from the inside out.

The flames flickered and glowed a hot orange red, the wood crackling as the rain continued to beat like a drum against the roof. The shower kicked on, and she imagined Brett standing beneath the water, naked and more virile than any man had a right to be.

It would have been romantic, if she wasn't so worried about Sam.

The door opened and Brett walked in, his jeans slung low on his lean hips, his chest bare, water still dotting the thick, dark chest hair. Her breath caught, her body ached, the need to be with him so strong that she felt limp from want and fear.

If she allowed herself to lean on him, she would fall apart when he left.

"Let me grab a shirt." He ducked into the bedroom, saving her from herself. But a light knock sounded on the door.

Assuming it was Maddox, or perhaps Ron, bringing Valeria and her daughter over, she walked over and opened the door.

A blond-haired woman in a short red dress and cowboy boots stood on the other side aiming a pistol at Willow's heart.

BRETT JAMMED HIS ARMS in his shirtsleeves, determined to dress before he wrapped Willow in his arms and dragged her to bed. She looked so sad and frightened and desolate on that couch. And her tear-swollen eyes when she'd emerged from the bathroom had torn him inside out.

He was buttoning the first button when he stepped back into the hallway and saw Kitty at the door. His heart began to pound. What was *she* doing here? How had she found him?

"Who…are you?" Willow whispered. "What do you want?"

Brett inched closer, shock hitting him at the sight of her fingers wrapped around that pistol. "Kitty? What the *hell* are you doing?"

Kitty waved the gun in Willow's face. "You *bitch*. You can't have Brett. He's mine."

Willow lifted her hands in surrender. "You… I saw your picture with Brett."

Brett gritted his teeth. The gossipmongers made it look as if he and Kitty were a hot item. That he was constantly entertaining women in hotels and his RV, even in the stables between rides. That he even indulged in orgies with women he met online and at the honky-tonks.

"You can't have him," Kitty screeched. "I love Brett and he loves me, don't you, sugar?"

Brett recognized the psycho look in Kitty's eyes. It was the same look she'd had the night she broke into his hotel room and he found her waiting in his bed, naked and oiled, crying and threatening suicide if he didn't marry her that night.

He inched closer, watching her for signs that she intended to fire that gun. "Kitty, it's all right. Just put down the pistol. This is not what you think."

She glared at him, then at Willow. "Not what it looks like? You're both half-naked and alone in this cabin." She waved the gun at Willow. "But you can't have him. Brett and I are meant to be together."

Willow lifted her chin. "Brett is just an old friend. Nothing is happening here. I swear."

Just an old friend? Was that how she saw him?

Kitty's hand trembled, and she fluffed her long blond curls with her free hand. "Is that true, Brett? She means nothing to you?"

Brett swallowed hard, and gave Willow a look that he hoped she understood. One that silently encouraged her to play along. "That's right. Willow and I knew each other in high school. I'm just helping her out with a problem."

Kitty moved forward, hips swaying as she curved one arm around Brett's neck. "Then you've told her about us?"

Brett kept his eyes on the gun.

"I saw the pictures of you two together, Kitty," Willow cut in. "You're a lucky girl to have Brett."

"No, I'm the lucky one." Brett lifted a hand to stroke Kitty's hair and pasted on his photo-ready smile. Even the times he'd been sick or bruised and half-dead from being thrown, he'd used that smile. "Come on, honey. Let's go outside and take a walk. I'll show you my ranch."

Kitty gave Willow a wry look as if to say she'd just won a victory, and Brett ushered Kitty toward the door. "You'll love Horseshoe Creek."

Kitty batted her lashes at him, her eyes full of stars. Or maybe she was high on drugs.

She leaned into him, and he stepped onto the porch with her, then escorted her down the steps. When they'd reached the landing, he made his move. He grabbed the gun from her, then twisted her arm behind her back, and pulled her against him so she couldn't move. "This is it, Kitty. You've gone too far."

She struggled to get away, but he kept a strong hold on her arm and yelled for Willow. The door screeched open, and Willow poked her head out.

"Brett?"

"Call Maddox," he said between gritted teeth. "She's going to jail."

WILLOW WAS STILL trembling when Maddox arrived. She tightened the belt on her robe and waited inside while Brett explained the situation to his brother.

The rain had died down enough for her to hear Brett's explanation through the window. "She's been stalking me for months, Maddox.

But tonight she went too far. She pulled a gun on Willow."

Kitty jerked against the handcuffs, her sobs growing louder. "How can you do this to me, to *us*, Brett. I love you! I thought we were going to get married!"

"We had two dates, that was it," Brett said to his brother. "I swear. I didn't lead her on, Maddox. There was never anything between us."

Maddox raised a brow. "Willow's here?"

Willow ducked behind the curtain. She didn't care if Maddox knew she was visiting Brett, but she didn't want to face him. He probably thought she was cheating on her husband with Brett.

Worse, if he asked questions about Leo, she didn't want to lie.

"Yes," Brett said. "But that's not what this is about. I need you to take Kitty into custody. Contact her family and tell them she needs psychiatric help."

Maddox hauled Kitty into the back of his police SUV. Tears streaked her face, and she was still screaming Brett's name as Maddox drove away.

Willow braced herself as Brett strode in. His hair was damp, his jaw rigid, that spark of flirtatiousness in his eyes gone. He looked angry and worried and...so damn masculine and sexy that her heart tripped.

"You've been breaking hearts everywhere you

go, haven't you, Brett?" She regretted the words the moment she said them. The bitter jealousy in her tone gave her feelings away.

THERE WAS NO way Brett was going to let Willow believe that he'd been in love with that deranged woman.

"Willow," he said, his teeth clenched. "I swear, we went out twice, then I realized she was unstable. After that, she started stalking me."

"I saw the pictures, Brett." Her voice cracked. "*Everyone* saw them."

He strode toward her, water dripping from his hair, his eyes luminous with emotions. "You can't believe everything you see in the tabloids. They're trying to sell copies."

"But you slept with her."

"Twice and I was half-drunk at the time. A week later, she broke into my hotel room and was waiting in my bed naked. When I told her to leave and pushed her out the hotel door, the press snapped a picture and turned it into something lurid."

Her eyes glittered with anger and something else…*jealousy*? Was it possible that Willow still cared for him?

"So all the pictures of you and the women were fake?"

His heart hammered as he closed the distance between them. He knew she was scared for her son and frustrated, and so was he. But he couldn't allow her to think that he didn't care. That he hadn't wanted her every damn day he was gone.

So he tilted her chin up and forced her to look into his eyes. "I wasn't a saint, Willow. But know this, I never kissed a woman without wishing she was you."

Then he did what he'd wanted to do ever since he'd ridden back into town.

He dragged her into his arms and kissed her with all the hunger he'd kept at bay for the past few years. Except this time he wouldn't stop at kissing as he had before. This time he wanted all of Willow.

Chapter Fifteen

Willow clung to Brett's words. None of those women had meant anything to him. When he'd closed his eyes, he'd seen her face.

Just as she had imagined Brett holding her when she was in Leo's arms.

Leo had known that she hadn't loved him. He'd felt it. Not that she had anything to feel guilty about. Apparently he'd never loved her either.

Of course he'd acted like he had. He'd showered her with attention and gifts and affection at a time when she'd been most vulnerable.

But it had all been a lie.

Brett's lips fused with hers, and she welcomed the sensations flooding her. Anything to soothe the pain and fear clawing at her heart.

Brett stroked her hair, then ran his hands down her back, pulling her closer to him so she felt the hard planes of his body against her curves. Her pulse raced, need and desire mingling with the desperateness that she'd felt since he'd walked back into her life.

He'd come the minute she'd called. Would he have come sooner if she'd had the courage to ask?

He made a low sound in his throat, and her hunger spiraled. "Willow, I want you," he said in a gruff whisper against her neck.

She tilted her head back, shivering at his breath on her skin. "I want you, too."

Brett swung her up into his arms and carried her to the bedroom. She kissed him frantically, urging him to do more, and he set her on her feet, then looked into her eyes.

"I've wanted you every day since I left Pistol Whip."

"I've wanted you, too, Brett." It had always been him. No one else. There never would be.

But her voice was lost as he nibbled at her lips again and drove his mouth against hers. They kissed, the passion growing hotter as he probed her mouth apart with his tongue. Lips and tongues mated and danced, his fingers trailing over her back, down to her waist, then one hand slid up to cup her breast.

Her breath caught and her nipple stiffened as he stroked her through her robe. She wanted him naked, touching and loving her everywhere.

Her whispered sigh was all the encouragement he needed. He cupped her face and looked into her eyes again, and for a second, the young boy she'd fallen in love with stood in his place.

All their dreams and fantasies, whispered loving words, kisses and secret rendezvous… She was back in the barn with Brett, hiding out with the boy she loved.

Then there was the night he'd come back to Pistol Whip. He'd shown up on her doorstep and she'd taken one look at him standing in the rain and invited him into her bed.

They'd made love as if they'd never been apart. They'd also made Sam that night.

Her robe fell to the floor, cool night air brushing her skin. His breath rasped out with appreciation as he cupped both breasts in his hands.

"You're so beautiful," he murmured.

She blushed at his blatant perusal, but shyness fled as he lowered his mouth and drew one stiff nipple into his mouth. Willow moaned as erotic sensations splintered through her, and she threaded her fingers in his hair, holding him close as he laved one breast, then the other.

Aching to touch him, she popped the first button on his shirt, then the second. He pulled away from her long enough to toss his shirt to the floor. His bare chest was broader than she remembered, dusted with dark hair, his skin bronzed from the sun, although a few scars lined his torso. She wondered how he'd gotten each one of them, but didn't ask. She didn't want to talk.

She wanted to be in his arms, loving him the way she once had when life had been simple and she'd had dreams of a future.

She unbuttoned his jeans, the sound rasping in the silence, and he kicked them off. Her body tingled as his hands skated over her hips. His eyes grew dark and needy, and he pulled her against him.

Her breasts felt heavy, achy, the tingling in her thighs and womb intensifying as he kissed her again and she shoved his boxers down his legs. Finally he stood naked in front of her. Powerful muscles flexed in his chest, arms and thighs, and his sex was thick and long, pulsing with excitement.

She trailed her fingers over his bare chest, and he moaned, then cradled her against him and walked them to the bed. Her head hit the pillow, her hair fanning out, as he nibbled at her neck again, then raked kisses along her neck and throat, moving down to her breasts where he loved her again until she begged for more.

NEED PULSED THROUGH Brett as he coaxed Willow onto the bed. His body ached for her, but the need to assuage her pain was just as strong.

He closed his mouth around one turgid nipple and suckled her, his sex hardening as she moaned his name. She stroked his calf with her foot, raking it up and down as she dug her hands into his hair.

Her hunger spiked his own, and he trailed sweet hungry kisses down her belly to her inner thighs.

"Brett…"

"*Shh*, just enjoy, baby." He flicked his tongue along her thigh, finding his way to the tender spot that made her go crazy. She tasted sweet and erotic, just as he remembered, and he teased her with his tongue until she clawed at his arms, begging him to come to her.

"I need you, Brett," Willow whispered.

He flicked his tongue over and over her tender nub until her body began to quiver and she cried out in release.

"Please, Brett."

Brett's heart pounded with the need to be inside her as he lifted himself and covered her with his body. For a moment, he lay on top of her savoring her tender curves against the hard planes of his chest and thighs. But she rubbed her hands down his back, then splayed them on his hips and butt, and his sex surged, needing more.

He tilted his head and looked into her passion-glazed eyes, then braced his body on his hands, and grabbed a condom from his jeans' pocket. She helped him roll it on, her fingers driving him insane as she touched his bare skin. When he had the protection in place, he kissed her again, deeply, hungrily, then rose above her and stroked her center with his erection. She groaned again, then slid her hand down and guided him home.

The moment he entered her, he closed his eyes and hesitated, forcing himself to slow down or he was going to explode. She lifted her hips and undulated them, inviting him to move inside her, and he did.

In and out, he thrust himself, filling her, stroking her with his length, pumping harder and faster as they built a natural rhythm. Sweat beaded on his forehead as he intensified their lovemaking, his release teetering on the edge.

Willow clutched at him, rubbing his back as she moved beneath him, then groaned his name as another orgasm claimed her. He kissed her again, then lifted her hips so he could move deeper inside her, so deep that he felt her core. She breathed his name against his neck.

It was the sweetest sound he'd ever heard, a sound he'd missed so much that it tipped him over the edge and his release splintered through him.

WILLOW CLOSED HER EYES and savored the feel of being in Brett's arms. Erotic sensations rocked through her with such intensity that she clung to him, emotions overwhelming her.

Tears burned the backs of her eyelids. She had

told herself not to fall in love with Brett again, but that had been futile.

Because she'd never stopped loving him.

Fear made her chest tighten again. She'd barely survived the first time he'd left her. How would she survive this time?

A deep sigh escaped her as he rolled them sideways and tucked her up against him. Brett kissed the top of her head, then disappeared into the bathroom for a moment. She thought he was going to dress and leave her alone, and she already missed him.

But he crawled back in bed with her, pulled her into his embrace and rubbed her arm. His body felt hot against hers as his breathing rasped out. She wanted to stay in his arms forever.

"Willow?"

She tensed, knowing she should confess the truth about Sam.

"I've been thinking. Wondering why Leo came to your house the day he died."

Willow went still. "I hoped he was going to drop the signed divorce papers by."

Brett took a strand of her hair between his fingers and stroked it the same way he had when they were young and in love. "But why that *particular* day? What if he really came back for the money? Maybe he retrieved it from the original place he'd buried it."

Willow turned to look into his eyes. "You think he had it with him that day?"

Brett shrugged. "Maybe he knew his partners were onto him, so he decided to hide it at your house. It wasn't in his truck. And we didn't find it where that map led us or at his mother's grave."

Willow's pulse kicked up, and she shoved the covers back. "Then we need to search my house."

Brett nodded, although before she slid from bed, he pulled her back and kissed her again. Her heart fluttered with love and hope.

When they found the money and Sam was home, would Brett forgive her for keeping her secret? Was it possible that they might be a family someday?

Her cell phone buzzed, and she startled. Sam?

Brett handed her the phone from the nightstand and she punched Connect. "Hello."

"Do you have the money?"

Panic shot through Willow. "No, but I think I know where it is."

"Where?"

She swallowed, struggling for courage. "Meet me at my house in an hour. Bring my son to me, and you can have it."

BRETT YANKED ON his jeans and shirt while Willow vaulted from bed and threw on her clothes.

He hoped to hell he was right, that the money was hidden somewhere at Willow's.

But just to be on the safe side, he grabbed the duffel bag he'd used to bring his clothes in, then packed some newspaper in the bottom.

"What are you doing?"

"If we don't find the money, I'll use this as a decoy until we rescue Sam." He retrieved his rifle from the corner in the den, wishing he had that money from his accounts to cover the newspaper, but hopefully they'd find Leo's money, and he wouldn't need this bag. And if they checked it...well, he had his rifle. He'd do whatever he had to do to get the boy.

He snatched his coat and handed Willow her jacket.

"Let's hurry. I want to look for the money before this bastard arrives." His phone buzzed, though, and he tensed. Maddox.

What if he'd somehow discovered Leo's body on the ranch?

Exhaling slowly, he punched Connect while Willow tugged on her jacket and boots. "Hey."

"Brett, what kind of trouble are you involved in?"

"I told you that woman was stalking me. End of story."

"I'm not talking about her," Maddox said sharply. "I want the truth about what you're doing. You're looking into Willow's husband, aren't you?"

Brett gritted his teeth. Did he know Leo was dead? "Why would you ask that?"

"I've been investigating a cattle-rustling ring that a man named Garcia is serving time for. It's his wife and kid you brought to the ranch, isn't it?"

He should have realized that would arouse Maddox's suspicions. "Maddox—"

"Just shut up and listen. I know you've always had a thing for Willow, and she's at that cabin with you. But her husband is dangerous."

"What do you know about him? Did he hurt her?"

"That's my guess. Dad talked to me one day and said he was worried, that something was off there."

If he'd been around, he would have known himself. And Willow never would have suffered.

Maddox cleared his throat. "He was in with some bad people. That's the reason you were looking up prison records, wasn't it?"

Brett glanced at his watch, impatient. "Yes, Maddox, but I have to go."

"Brett, let me handle the situation. I think Howard was involved with those cattle rustlers. I don't have proof but I'll get it. In fact, I'm trying to locate him to question him now. Does Willow know where he is, Brett? Because if she's covering for him, she could go to jail, too."

Willow looked panicked and tugged him toward the door. "I'll tell her if she hears from him to call you."

He didn't wait on a response. He hung up with a curse. Maddox was smart; it wouldn't take him long to figure out what was going on.

Willow followed him outside where the rain was still beating on the roof as they hurried to his truck.

Wind and rain battered the windshield as he drove, blurring his vision of the road. He flipped the wipers to High, his nerves on edge as he turned onto Willow's road.

The truck bounced over the ruts, mud spewing. He looked over his shoulder to make sure no one was following.

Hell, for all he knew, Maddox might be on his tail.

Willow twisted in the seat, obviously agitated. "They *will* bring Sam, won't they?"

Brett's gut contorted. He'd wondered the same thing.

If Sam could identify them, they might have already ditched him, then planned to take the money and run.

His fingers curled around the rifle on the seat beside him. If they had hurt Willow's little boy, he'd kill the bastards.

WILLOW SCANNED THE OUTSIDE of her house in case the kidnappers had arrived early. Her throat ached from holding back tears.

She was going to see Sam again. She had to see him.

But what if she and Brent were walking into a trap? What if they'd never intended to give her back her son?

Fear almost paralyzed her. Determined not to give up, though, she forced the terror at bay. She had to stay strong.

Brett parked and got out, carrying his rifle and the duffel bag with him. Memories of finding Leo dead in her bedroom flashed behind her eyes, and nausea climbed her throat. But she forged on, determined to hold it together.

They slogged through the rain and she unlocked the door, her shoulders knotted with anxiety. The den looked just as she'd left it, and so did the kitchen.

Although it felt as if it had been years since she'd been home. She didn't know if she could ever live here again.

"I don't know where he would have hidden it," Willow said.

"I'll search the closets. You search the kitchen. He could have taped an envelope with a key to a safety deposit box under a drawer or table."

Brett strode to the hall closet and began to dig

through it. She checked the cabinet and drawers in the kitchen and the desk, under the drawers and table, and on top of the cabinets. The laundry room came next. Her movements were harried as she ripped through plastic storage containers and checked beneath and behind the washer and dryer.

She searched the pantry, but yielded nothing, so she hurried to the bedrooms. Brett was in her room. The sight of the bloodstains was still so stark that it made her stomach turn.

Sucking in a sharp breath, she darted into Sam's room. Sam's toys and clothes were still scattered about as they'd left them. Knowing time was of the essence, she dropped to her knees and searched beneath the bed. Her hand connected with a toy superhero and she pulled it out, along with several odd socks, a ball and a candy wrapper.

Her thoughts raced as she pulled down his covers and checked below his mattress, the bottom of the box spring and the back of the headboard.

Panic was starting to tear at her, and she threw the closet door open and searched the floor. Shoes, toys and a cereal box. On the top shelf she found the extra blankets and sheets she'd folded along with a flashlight, Sam's Halloween costume and boxes of rocks they'd collected at the creek.

She dug through the corner of the closet and found a stack of magazines—rodeo magazines. Her throat closed as she spotted a picture of Brett on the front of one of them. He must have found this in her nightstand drawer.

"Any luck, Willow?" Brett's voice jerked her from her thoughts and she stuffed the magazines back inside.

"No, nothing. You?"

Brett scowled. "No, but I'm going to look around outside."

"I'll check the attic."

He nodded and she rushed to the hall and climbed in the attic while he stepped outside. The rain had slackened, although droplets pinged off the window where the wind shook it from the trees.

Several boxes of old clothing and quilt scraps were stored on one wall. She went to the antique wardrobe and opened it. It would be a perfect hiding place. In fact, Sam had hidden inside it once when they were playing hide-and-seek. After that, she'd made sure that it couldn't be locked so he wouldn't get trapped.

She swung the door open and found fabric scraps from her projects along with boxes of photographs of her and Brett in high school.

But there was no money anywhere.

Outside an engine rumbled in the distance, and

she looked out the attic window and saw lights flickering. Was it them?

Did they have Sam?

BRETT FOUND NOTHING in the garage, so he scanned the side of the house for a crawl space or a hiding place but didn't see one.

The sound of the car engine made his nerves spike. He hurried inside and grabbed the rifle along with the duffel bag. Willow raced down the steps from the attic and clutched his arm. "Brett, what are we going to do?"

"Play along with me."

She nodded, although terror filled her eyes. Brett stepped onto the porch, deciding to use the darkness to camouflage the bag. A black sedan pulled up, lights turned off.

He held the rifle beside him, hand ready to draw, the duffel bag in his other hand. Willow's nervous breathing rattled in the quiet.

The sedan door opened and a man wearing a ski mask stepped from the backseat. The driver remained behind the wheel, hidden in the shadows.

The silver glint of metal flickered against the night. "The woman needs to bring the money over here."

"First, we see the boy," Brett said in a tone that brooked no argument.

A hesitation. The wind hurled rain onto the porch and caused a twig to snap and fall in front of the man. He didn't react, except to reach inside the car and snatch something.

Brett feared it was another weapon, but a little boy wearing a jacket appeared, his body shaking. He couldn't see his face well for the shadows, but he cried out for Willow.

"Mommy!"

Willow stepped onto the porch. *"Sam!* Honey, I'm here. Are you all right?"

"I wanna come home!" Sam yelled.

Brett caught Willow, before she barreled forward.

"Send the boy over, then I'll throw you the money," Brett ordered.

A nasty chuckle echoed from the man. "No way. The woman brings the money. When I see it, I release the kid."

Brett's fingers tightened around the rifle. He was a damn good shot. But this was a dangerous game.

Willow's and her son's lives depended on him.

"Fine." Willow grabbed the duffel bag.

"Willow?" Brett reached for her but she shook off his hand.

"I have to do this," Willow said. "I'll do anything for Sam."

Brett's gut churned as she slowly walked down the steps.

"Send the boy," Brett said.

The man took Sam by the collar and half dragged him across the yard. Brett inched down a step, but the man aimed the gun at Willow.

"Stay put, McCullen, or they're both dead."

Chapter Sixteen

Willow soaked up the sight of her little boy's features.

His dark eyes were big and terrified, but he was alive. And she didn't see any visible injuries or bruises.

"Are you okay, honey?" she asked softly as she approached Sam.

He gave a little nod of his head, but his chin quivered. "I wanna come home."

"You *are* coming home," Willow assured him. There was no way this man would leave with her son. She'd die first.

The man's gun glinted as she neared him, but that ski mask disguised his face.

Willow clutched the duffel bag to her side. "I have what you came for. Now let my son go."

The man glanced down at the bag. "Closer."

Willow inched forward, but kept the bag slightly behind her, determined to lure Sam away before the man realized the bag was empty.

She hesitated a few inches from him, then stood ramrod straight, her chin lifted. "Let him go."

The man met her gaze, then shoved Sam. "Go on, kid." At the same time, he reached for the bag.

"Mommy!" Sam ran toward her, and she hugged him to her and threw the bag at the man's feet a few inches from him.

She gripped Sam by the arm just as he ripped open the bag to check the contents. "Run back to the house, Sam!"

He was crying and clinging to her, and she turned to run with him, but the man lunged at her and snatched her arm. "You lying bitch."

"Run, Sam, *run*!" Her head snapped back as the man caught her.

Brett was coming down the steps, his rifle aimed. "Let her go!"

Sam stumbled and fell, crying out for her. "Mommy!"

"Save him," Willow shouted to Brett.

The second man in the car fired his gun, and Brett jumped back slightly, then pressed his hand on his left shoulder. Blood began to ooze out and soak his shirt.

He'd been shot.

"Please let me go," Willow cried. "I don't have your money, and my son needs me."

"Shut up." The man jammed the gun to her head, but Brett started forward again so the man spoke to Brett. "Move another inch and I'll shoot her."

Brett kept his rifle aimed, but froze a few feet from Sam. "Listen, man, she tried to find the money. But she doesn't know where it is."

A litany of curse words filled the air. Sam pushed up from the ground and shook his little fists at the man. "Let my mommy go!"

Sam started to run back toward her, but Brett snatched him by the neck of his jacket. "Stay still, son. I'll handle this."

The man kept the gun to her head and dragged her back toward the sedan. She wanted to fight, but the cold barrel against her temple warned her not to mess with him. She didn't want to die and leave Sam motherless.

Sam was sobbing, so Brett picked him up. Willow saw the moment he looked into Sam's face and realized he was his.

His gaze flew to hers, questions mingling with shock.

The driver of the sedan fired at Brett's feet, though, and he dodged the bullet, protecting Sam with his body.

The kidnapper opened the sedan door. Willow shoved at him, but he grabbed her around the throat, then pressed the barrel of the gun to her head again.

"Don't hurt her. I'll get you some money!"

Brett shouted. "I have a hundred thousand of my own I'll give you in exchange for her."

"Get it and we'll talk." The man shoved Willow inside the car.

Willow tried to crawl across the seat to escape out the opposite door, but he slammed the gun against the back of her head, and the world went black.

BRETT'S HEART WAS pounding so loudly, he could hear the blood roaring in his ears. The driver of the sedan spun the vehicle around. The other man fired at Brett again to keep him from chasing them, and Brett clutched Sam and darted behind a tree to protect him.

"Mommy!" Sam screamed as the sedan accelerated. *"Mommy!"*

A cold knot of fear enveloped Brett as the sedan disappeared with Willow inside.

Sam wrapped his arms around Brett's neck and clung to him, his little body trembling with fear.

Sam. *His son.*

The words echoed over and over in his head. Sam was his little boy.

All this time, these years, the past few days— Willow hadn't told him. Had kept the truth from him.

Why? Because she thought he wouldn't have been a good father...

"I want my mommy!" Sam sobbed.

Brett patted the little boy's back, his heart aching for the ordeal Sam had suffered. For the fear and trauma, for the murder he'd witnessed.

And now his mother was gone, snatched at gunpoint in front of his eyes.

He pressed Sam's head to his shoulder and rocked him in his arms. "*Shh*, son, it'll be all right."

"My…mommy…"

Sam's sniffles punctuated the air, wrenching Brett's heart. "I know you're scared, son, and you've been through a lot." Brett's shoulder was starting to throb, and blood soaked his shirt. "But I'm here now. I'm here and I'll make things right."

I'm your father, he started to say. But he didn't want to confuse Sam now. Besides, what had Willow told him?

Sam thought that bastard Leo was his dad…

Rage heated Brett's blood. He would rectify *that* as soon as possible. As soon as he brought Willow home.

Then they would sit down and have a damn long talk.

Sam's cries softened, but his fingers dug into Brett's neck as Brett walked toward his pickup. He needed to take care of the bullet in his shoulder before he passed out. If he did, he wouldn't be any good to Sam or Willow.

They were his priority now.

But how was he going to remove this bullet

without seeing a doctor or drawing suspicion from the law?

He carried Sam around to the passenger side of the truck, his lungs squeezing for air when Sam looked up at him with those big eyes. Eyes that looked exactly like his. The cleft in his chin, the dimple…he was a McCullen through and through.

How had he not seen it before?

Because you didn't look.

In the photo he'd seen of Sam, the boy was wearing a cowboy hat. It had hurt too much for him to think about Willow having another man's son, so he hadn't paid attention to the child's features.

But this boy was *his*.

He fastened Sam's seat belt, soaking up his face for a moment, and thinking about what he'd missed. All those baby years. The first time he'd walked. Christmases and birthdays…

Sam wiped at his nose and looked up at Brett. The fear there nearly stalled Brett's heart. "You helping those mean men?" Sam whispered.

Brett nearly choked on a sharp denial. But he didn't want to scare Sam any more than he already was. "No, son." He gently raked a hand over the child's hair, emotions nearly overwhelming him. "I'm a friend of your mommy's. I've been helping her try to get you back from those men."

Sam's eyes narrowed as he looked at Brett's shoulder. "They shot you like they shot Daddy."

Leo was not his father. But Sam *had* witnessed the murder. "Yes, but I'm not going to die, Sam. And I'm not going to leave you." Not ever again. "I'm going to get your mother back. I promise."

Sam's chin quivered, but he gave Brett a brave nod.

Knowing time was working against him, he walked around to the driver's side and climbed in. He reached inside his pocket and removed a handkerchief, then jammed it inside his shirt over the wound to help stem the blood flow.

Then he cranked the truck and drove back toward Horseshoe Creek.

He was starting to feel weak, and he needed help. Someone to remove this damn bullet and someone to watch Sam, so he could get hold of that cash and trade it for Willow's life.

He didn't know where to go. Who to turn to.

Maddox would be furious when he found out what Brett had done.

But he was the only one who could help him now.

He'd probably lock Brett up when all was said and done.

He glanced over at Sam who was watching him with those big sad eyes.

But Sam was his son, and if there was anything that Maddox cared about, it was family.

Brett would pay the consequences when this was over and go to jail if it came to that.

But he'd save Willow first.

WILLOW STIRRED FROM UNCONSCIOUSNESS, but her head was spinning and nausea rose to her throat. She lifted her hand to the back of her head and felt blood. The car bounced over the rocky road, jarring her and making her feel ill.

She struggled to sit up, but the car veered to the right, throwing her against the side.

"Be still, bitch, or you're going to get it again."

A sob welled inside her, but she sucked it down. "Please let me go. My little boy needs me."

He barked a sinister laugh. "You're the one who screwed up. You should have given me the money instead of getting greedy."

Willow pushed herself to a sitting position. "I'm not *greedy*. I told you I didn't know where the money was and I *don't*."

He grabbed her arm, clenching it so tightly that pain shot through her arm and shoulder. "We know Leo came to see you, that he took the money from where he'd first hidden it. He was supposed to meet us that day with it, but he stopped off at your house first."

"Leo and I have been separated for years,"

Willow cried. "He came by to drop off divorce papers, not give me money."

"Because you were already keeping it for him," the man snarled.

Willow shook her head back and forth. How could she convince them that she was telling the truth?

And what if she did and they killed her because she was of no use to them anymore?

Then she'd never see Sam again, and he would grow up without a mother...

She closed her eyes and said a prayer. Even if she didn't make it, Brett had recognized that he had a son. He would raise Sam as a McCullen.

Sam will be all right.

Except she wanted to be there to see him grow up, to learn to ride a horse, to play ball and graduate from school and get married one day...

BRETT IGNORED THE PAIN in his shoulder and focused on driving back to the ranch. He had to get Sam to Horseshoe Creek where he'd be safe.

Dark clouds hovered above, threatening more rain, and he took a curve too quickly and nearly lost control. Sam's little face looked pale in the dark, and Brett reached out and squeezed his shoulder.

"I know you've been through it, little man,

and you miss your mother, but hang in there a little longer."

"You said you knew her?" Sam said in a small voice.

"Yes," Brett said. "We were friends back in high school." *Friends and lovers. And I'm your father.*

Although Sam obviously had no idea.

Sam suddenly tilted his head to the side. "You're that rodeo star aren't you? I saw your picture in that magazine Mommy had."

Willow had a magazine with his picture in it.

Of course she had. She'd seen pictures of him and Kitty. She thought he was sleeping with a different woman every night.

And he had, he admitted silently.

But would he have if he'd known he had a child? That Willow had delivered his baby?

Regret and heartache ballooned inside him as he turned onto the road leading back to Horseshoe Creek.

Sam sat up straighter, his little face turned toward the window. "Where are you taking me?"

The poor kid had been kidnapped. He probably was wondering what Brett was going to do to him. "We're going to my ranch," Brett said. "Your mommy likes it there. And I have two brothers and a nice lady named Mama Mary who took care of me when I was little. She'll take care of you till your mommy is home."

As soon as he said the words, he felt better. Maddox would be angry, but Mama Mary would love Sam unconditionally with no questions asked.

"You gots horses?"

Brett's mouth twitched. "Yes, buddy. Do you know how to ride?"

"Not really." Sam's voice dropped to a low whisper. "Mommy said I was too little."

Brett rubbed his hand over Sam's head again. "Well, you look pretty big to me. And I know you're tough. So I'll teach you to ride soon. Sound good?"

Sam nodded, and for a moment, Brett saw himself when he was little. Anytime he was upset or mad, he'd ridden across the ranch and the world had seemed better. He could pass that on to his son.

The farmhouse slid into view, and for once, he was relieved to see Maddox's SUV in front of the house. He parked, pressing his hand to his bloody shoulder as he hurried around to help Sam.

The little boy took his hand and jumped to the ground, and Brett held on to him as they walked up the porch steps. When he opened the door, Maddox was standing in the hall, his expression dark.

"Brett, I need to talk to you. This evening I found something—"

Brett cut him off. He had to get the words out fast. "I have to talk to you, too." Brett swayed slightly, his head light from blood loss.

Maddox's gaze took in Sam, then he noticed Brett's bloody shoulder. "Good grief, you've been shot."

Brett nodded and stumbled forward, and Maddox caught him. "It's worse, Maddox. I need your help. Two men...they kidnapped Willow."

Chapter Seventeen

Willow struggled against the bindings around her wrists and feet as the man tossed her into a dark room. A sliver of light managed to peek through the curtains, and she dragged herself on her belly to the bed and slowly clawed her way on top of it.

She pushed the curtain aside, and hoped to escape through the window, but it was nailed shut.

A sob welled in her throat, and she slumped back down on the bed. Was this the room where they'd kept Sam?

She mentally searched for strength. If her little boy had held it together long enough for her to save him, she could do it long enough for Brett to find her.

The most important thing was that Sam was safe.

Safe with his father who probably hated her now for keeping his son from him all these years.

That didn't matter either, not now. Sam was okay and if she died tonight, Brett would take care of Sam. He'd teach him how to play baseball and skip stones in the creek behind the ranch, and how to saddle a horse and trick ride.

Although one day he might teach him to ride a bull and she wasn't so sure about that.

She would miss it all if she was dead, but Sam would be happy with his father. He would raise him to be an honorable, brave McCullen man.

She rolled to her side on the bed and looked across the room. A ratty stuffed animal lay on the floor, along with a piece of rope.

Sam had been here. He'd twisted the rope into the letter *S*. Her heart warmed as she remembered him pretending to rope cattle like the cowboys on TV.

Brett would teach him how to rope calves one day, too.

She wanted to be there for him and see all those things.

She blinked, and struggled to untie her hands, but the ropes cut into her wrists. Frustrated, she drew her knees up and tried to reach her ankles with her hands to untie her feet, but the knot was so tight, she couldn't budge it.

Outside, footsteps pounded and voices echoed through the wall. She forced herself to be very still so she could hear, although it was difficult over the sound of her own roaring heart.

"You took the woman now? What the hell are you doing?"

Willow tensed. That was a woman's voice. It sounded familiar, but it was too muffled for her to place.

"I thought she was lying about the money."

"But what if she doesn't know where it is?"

"That cowboy said he'll pay us. It won't be half a million, but it'll be enough to get out of the country so we can lie low for a while."

"All right. But give the man a deadline. The longer you wait, the more likely we are going to get caught."

"Twenty-four hours. That's the deadline. If he doesn't produce the money by then, kill her."

BRETT'S KNEES FELT like they were going to cave in.

"Brett, who shot you?" Maddox caught him just before he collapsed. "Mama Mary, Rose, hurry, I need help!"

Sam was still clinging to Brett, looking scared to death.

"It's okay, son," Brett murmured in a soothing voice as he lowered him to the floor. "I'll be fine. Maddox is my brother." He gestured toward the badge on Maddox's shirt. "He's a good guy, the sheriff. He'll help us find your mommy and get rid of those bad men."

Mama Mary and Rose rushed in, both startled by the blood on his shirt.

"Oh, my word!" Mama Mary cried. "What's going on?"

"This is Willow's son, Sam," Brett said. *And my son, too.*

"Brett, this is Rose," Maddox said.

Brett muttered that he was glad to meet her. "Take care of Sam, Mama Mary. Two men took Willow and I need Maddox's help."

Rose gasped. "They took Willow?"

"You know her?" Brett asked.

Rose nodded. "I sell her quilts at my antiques shop."

Mama Mary dropped to her knees, her big bulk swaying as she rubbed Sam's arms. "Come on, little one. I bet you're hungry and tired aren't you?"

Sam hung on to Brett's leg. "I want my mommy," Sam said in a haunted voice.

Tears glistened on Mama Mary's eyelashes, but she didn't hesitate to comfort Sam, just the way she'd comforted him when he was little and his mother died.

"I know you do, sugar," Mama Mary said. "And don't you worry. Mr. Brett and Mr. Maddox are the two finest men in Wyoming. They'll have your mama back in no time." She dried his eyes with her apron. "Now your mama would want you to eat."

Sam leaned in to the big woman's loving arms. "Come on, little one. Mama Mary will whip you up some mac and cheese. I bet you like mac and cheese, don't you? It was Mr. Brett's favorite when he was your age."

Sam nodded against her, and Brett ruffled Sam's hair. "It's okay, bud. I'll be right here. My brother's going to patch me up."

Sam seemed to accept what he'd said, and Mama Mary carted him to the kitchen where Brett knew he was in good hands.

Maddox helped him into the den and onto the couch. "Rose, get some towels so we can stop this bleeding. Then call Dr. Cumberland. We have to remove this bullet."

"There's no time," Brett argued.

"Listen to me, Brett," Maddox said in a deep voice. "You won't be any good if you die on me."

Rose dashed from the room, and Maddox poured two whiskeys. He returned and handed Brett a glass, then took a swig of his own, his eyes dark with rage and worry.

"Now, what the *hell* is going on?"

Brett rubbed his hand over his eyes, then swallowed his drink. "You aren't going to like it."

"I know that." Maddox walked over and sat down beside him. "But I'm your brother, man. And if you need my help, I'm here. But I need to know everything."

Brett nearly choked on his emotions. He'd just

found out he had a son. And now his brother was ready to help him.

Of course Maddox didn't know what all he'd done.

But it was time for him to come clean. He'd take whatever punishment came his way. As long as Maddox helped him save Willow.

"The night of the funeral," he began, "Willow called me, hysterical."

Maddox leaned his elbows on his knees. "This has to do with her husband, Leo, doesn't it? Did she know he was a crook?"

Brett shook his head, a bead of perspiration trickling down his brow. "They were separated, but he was supposed to come by her house and drop off divorce papers. On the way he picked up Sam. When Willow arrived home, she found Leo dead. And the men who'd killed him had abducted Sam."

Maddox muttered a curse, and let a heartbeat of silence pass. "Go on."

"They told Willow that if she called the law, they'd kill Sam."

"That's the reason you were snooping around on my computer?"

"Yes. The kidnappers said that Leo had a half million dollars. They wanted the money in exchange for her son." *His* son.

"What's the connection with the prisoner?"

"I think the kidnappers worked with Leo, they were his partners and he betrayed them so they killed him."

"His partners? You're talking about the cattle-rustling ring?"

"Yeah. When the police became suspicious about it, the leaders threatened Garcia's family, so he took the fall for all the charges."

Rose ran in with some towels, and Maddox cut Brett's shirt off to examine the wound. They pressed towels to the bloody area, then applied pressure.

"So where's Leo's body?" Maddox asked.

Brett gritted his teeth at the pain. "I buried him, Maddox. Just until we could find Sam."

Maddox exploded and stormed across the room. Rose offered Brett a sympathetic look, folded another towel and pressed it to his bloody shoulder.

Brett cleared his throat. "I'm sorry, Maddox, but I didn't know what else to do. I did try to preserve evidence."

"How could you preserve evidence when you buried him?" Maddox crossed his arms as he stopped pacing. "Brett, do you realize what kind of position you've put me in?"

Brett let the silence fall. He could never live up to Maddox.

"Yes, and I'm sorry," he said honestly. "But

Willow was terrified, afraid they'd kill Sam because we think he witnessed Leo's murder."

Maddox pinched the bridge of his nose.

Brett's lungs squeezed for air. "There's something else."

Maddox shoved his hands through his hair. "What?"

Brett swallowed hard. He couldn't believe it himself. But it was true. "Sam is my son."

WILLOW CLENCHED THE PIECE of rope that she'd found on the floor in her hand as if that piece of cord tied her to Sam.

She picked up the stuffed animal and pressed it to her nose. Sam's sweet little-boy smell permeated the toy just as his infectious laugh and insatiable curiosity filled her with love.

Footsteps echoed outside, then the door squeaked open. Remembering they'd set a deadline before they killed her, she barely suppressed tears.

They had removed their bandannas this time, revealing harsh faces, rough with beard stubble and scars. Faces that were now imprinted in her brain.

Which meant they were definitely going to kill her.

The bigger man with beefy hands strode over to her with a gun in his hand. The taller one stepped into the room with his phone.

The bigger guy grabbed her by her hair and jammed the weapon to her head. Willow cried out at the force, but froze when she felt the cold barrel at her temple.

Were they going to kill her now?

BRETT GRITTED HIS TEETH as the doctor removed the bullet, then cleaned the wound and stitched his shoulder.

"I didn't know doctors made house calls anymore." Although he knew this man had taken care of his father and had been friends with Joe McCullen.

Dr. Cumberland chuckled, but his eyes looked serious beneath his square glasses. "I usually *don't*, but this is a small town, and your brother is the sheriff."

"Yeah."

"He's a good man," the doctor said. "He takes care of this town and the people in it."

Guilt nagged at Brett. Unfortunately, Brett had put him in a terrible position.

From the doorway he heard Maddox discussing the situation with Rose. "I know he had reason," Maddox said, "but this is a mess. I have to retrieve Howard's body and have the crime scene processed."

"What about Willow?"

Maddox made a low sound in his throat. "We'll figure out a way to find her."

Dr. Cumberland handed Brett two prescription bottles. "Take these for pain when you need them. The other is an antibiotic to prevent infection."

Brett waved Maddox over. "I've already called my business manager. He should have a hundred thousand ready for me by morning."

Maddox scowled down at him where he lay on the couch. "Okay, but even if you give them the money, they may still kill Willow."

Brett clenched the pill bottles in one hand. "I won't let that happen."

Maddox studied him for a long moment while Rose watched, her expression concerned. "I want these guys," Maddox said. "Leo Howard was a crook. He was the leader of a cattle-rustling operation across the state. Our town isn't the first one he hit."

"Willow didn't know anything about it," Brett said earnestly.

"I don't doubt that. But he even stole from Horseshoe Creek, Brett. So this is personal."

More personal to Brett because the man had threatened Willow and Sam.

"Do you know who Leo was working with?" Maddox asked.

Brett thought hard. "There was a man named Wally Norman who was questioned about the cattle rustling."

Maddox nodded. "Yeah. Norman went to prison later on other charges. I think his partner was a man named Jasper Day. Day disappeared after Norman was locked up. I suspect he was lying low until the heat died down and he could get his hands on his share."

"I think Boyle Gates might have been involved, too," Brett said. "Willow and I talked to him, but he threw us out."

"Gates?" Maddox pulled his hand down his chin. "I wondered how that SOB grew his spread so quickly. Probably filled it with stolen cattle."

"He's smart, though," Brett said. "If he's involved, he helped set Gus Garcia up to take the fall." He tried to sit up, but he swayed slightly. Maddox steadied him, and Brett set the pills on the table. He didn't intend to take anything to impair his judgment. He needed a clear head to save Willow.

"I'll send a team to process Willow's house," Maddox said. "If we can match prints to whoever was there, maybe we can use it to track down the men who have Willow. Knowing their identities may lead us to a location where they're holding her."

Maddox reached for his phone. "I'll also get my deputy looking into Day's and Norman's whereabouts."

Brett started to thank Maddox, but his phone buzzed. His shoulder throbbed as he shifted and dug it from his jacket pocket. A text.

Fear ripped through him at the sight of the

photo of Willow with the gun to her temple. Below the picture, the kidnapper had typed a message.

Twenty-four hours or she's dead.

Chapter Eighteen

Brett wanted to punch something. If those jerks hurt Willow, he'd *kill* them.

Maddox yanked on his jacket. "I'm meeting my head CSI guy, Hoberman, at Willow's. If the kidnappers left prints, we'll find them and get an ID."

Brett gripped the edge of the sofa to stand. "I'll go with you."

Maddox laid a hand on Brett's shoulder. "No, Brett. Let me do my job. You aren't going to be any good to anyone, if you don't get some rest."

Maddox leaned over and planted a kiss on Rose's lips. "I'll be back later."

"Be careful," Rose said softly.

Maddox's eyes darkened as he kissed her again, and Brett looked away.

He'd always seen his brother as the strong one, the one who didn't need anyone, but watching him with Rose gave him a glimpse of another side.

Maddox was just as vulnerable as he and Ray had been. Only Maddox had been the oldest, and his father had relied on him to be strong for his little brothers.

No wonder Maddox had resented the two of them when they let him down.

Mama Mary appeared at the door with Sam by her side. The gleam in the older woman's eyes told Brett all he needed to know. She'd fallen in love with the little boy at first sight.

Mama Mary was fierce and loving, had steered him back on track a few times when he'd strayed, but she always did it with a loving hand.

His heart twisted as his gaze rested on his son. His chin, those eyes, the dimple, even that cowlick reminded him of himself. And Sam looked just as lost as he had when his mother died.

But he was not going to let Sam lose Willow. Not as long as he had a breath in his body.

"Mr. Brett, he wolfed down that mac and cheese, but I believe this boy needs some sleep. I'm gonna take him upstairs. Which room do you want him in?"

Brett smiled at Mama Mary and pushed himself to stand. "My room. I'll take him."

Mama Mary's eyes twinkled with understanding. "There's a box of some of your old clothes in the storage room. I bet I could find some pajamas in there that would fit Sam."

"That would be great." Brett's shoulder throbbed as he made his way over to Sam, but he ignored the pain. "Come on, buddy. I'll show you my room."

Sam gave Brett a brave nod and slipped his small hand into Brett's.

Emotions flooded Brett.

A pity that now he'd come home, Brett's father was gone. And that Sam would never know his grandfather.

Sam tightened his fingers inside Brett's palm, and he squeezed his son's hand, amazed at the protective instincts that surged to life.

He would not let his kid down.

Together they climbed the steps, Brett walking slower to accommodate Sam's shorter stride. When they reached the landing, he took Sam to the last room on the right, his old bedroom.

Sam's eyes widened when he entered. Brett felt a sense of pride at the fact that his father had left all his rodeo posters on the walls. Men who'd been heroes to Brett and inspired his drive to join the circuit.

"Did you go to all those rodeos?" Sam asked.

Brett grinned. "Every last one. My daddy took me when I was little. And I'll take you."

Sam looked up at him in awe. "I wanna go, but Mommy always said no."

Brett stooped down to Sam's eye level and rubbed his arm. "Well, maybe together we can change her mind." Although hurt and anger with

Willow gnawed at him—she'd deprived him of the first four years of Sam's life.

He pushed aside his own feelings, though. Sam would have to come first.

"You really think she'll let me come to one of your rodeos?"

To *one* of his? "I promise we'll work something out. Maybe I can teach you some tricks one day. Would you like that?"

Sam bobbed his head up and down, fighting a yawn.

Mama Mary appeared with a pair of flannel pajamas with superheroes on them. "I think these will fit."

Brett took them from her and thanked her. "Will these do, little man?"

Sam nodded and began to peel off his jeans. Brett squatted down to help him change, worried as he looked for bruises on the boy. "Sam, I know you were scared of those bad men. Did they hurt you?"

Sam pulled on the pajamas. "They locked me in that dark room and wouldn't let me out."

The quiver in his voice tore at Brett. He helped Sam slide on the pajama shirt, then folded down the quilt, and Sam crawled into bed. Then he sat down beside him and tucked the covers up over Sam.

"Do you know where you were? Was it a

house or a barn? Was it in town or on a farm somewhere?"

Sam sniffed. "It was a house, but the windows was nailed shut."

Anger made Brett clench his jaw. "When you looked out the window, what did you see? Another building? Cows or horses?"

Sam twisted the sheet with his fingers. "Woods. There was trees and trees everywhere."

Brett sighed. "How about noises? Did you hear anything nearby? Maybe a train or cars? Or a creek?"

Sam scrunched his nose in thought. "I can't remember. I just heard that big man's mean voice. He tolded me to eat this gross sandwich, but I didn't want it, I wanted Mommy. And he got mad…"

Sam's voice broke and tears filled his eyes.

Brett held his breath. "What did he do when he got mad?"

"He yelled and throwed the food, and then he shut the door and locked me back up."

Brett hated the bastard more than he'd hated anyone in his life, but he softened his tone. "It's over now, little man. You'll never have to see those men again."

Sam collapsed into his arms again, and Brett rocked him back and forth, soothing him until the little boy's breathing steadied. He eased him back down on the bed and tucked him in again.

Sam's sleepy eyes drifted to the shelf, and Brett saw the stuffed pony he'd slept with as a boy. He took it down and handed it to Sam.

"This was my best friend when I was your age. His name is Lucky. He gets lonely up here. Can he sleep with you?"

Sam nodded, then took the pony, rolled to his side and tucked it under his arm. Brett planted a kiss on his head, his heart filled with overwhelming love.

"Night, little man."

Tomorrow he had to bring Willow home to his son.

But Willow hadn't told him about Sam, because she obviously thought he wouldn't make a good father.

How would she feel about letting him be part of Sam's life now?

WILLOW STRUGGLED AND FOUGHT to untie her hands and feet. Her fingers and wrists were raw, her nails jagged from trying to tear the rope in two. Finally, she fell into an exhausted sleep just before dawn.

But she dreamed Leo was standing over her with blood spewing from his chest while he held a gun against Sam's head. She motioned for Sam to stay still and begged Leo to let him go, but he waved the gun at her and ordered her to get on her knees and crawl outside.

Terrified for Sam, she did as he said. He shoved and kicked her until she reached the grave he'd dug for her. A sliver of moonlight illuminated the deep hole where snakes hissed and crawled along the edges, their tongues flicking out as if waiting to take a bite out of her.

Then Leo kicked her hard and she fell, tumbling down, fighting and clawing as she tasted dirt and the snakes slithered over her body and bit her, poison shooting through her blood as she screamed.

A man's loud voice boomeranged through the room as he burst through the door. Willow jerked upright, disoriented.

Reality quickly interceded as he rammed his face into hers. "Shut up or I'll shut you up."

Willow bit her tongue. She'd obviously been screaming in her sleep.

She sucked in a breath and stared at him, determined not to show fear.

Tense seconds passed as he glared at her, daring her to make a sound.

More footsteps, then the thinner man appeared. "We need to set up the meet."

"I'll handle it."

Willow shivered as they slammed the door and left her tied up and alone again. Terrified they'd kill her even if Brett found the money, she started to work on the knots again.

If she could just free herself, when one of them came in again, maybe she could get past him and run.

BRETT DOZED FOR a couple of hours, but couldn't sleep for worrying about Willow. Every hour that passed intensified his fear that he wouldn't be able to save her.

He called first thing about the money, and his manager said all he had to do was pick it up at the bank in Pistol Whip. Brett took a quick shower and checked on Sam, but he was still sleeping, so he grabbed a cup of coffee and breakfast.

Maddox came in, looking tired and stressed to the hilt.

"My manager called. I'm meeting him at the bank to pick up the cash he liquidated for me," Brett told him.

Maddox accepted a cup of coffee from Mama Mary, then joined Brett at the table. "We found prints at Willow's. Jasper Day's and Wally Norman's. Norman escaped prison last week. He shanked a guard and killed him, then took his uniform to escape. We believe he contacted Day and they came hunting Howard."

"And when Leo refused to give them their share of the profit from the stolen cattle, they killed him."

"Exactly."

"And Willow and Sam got caught up in it because she married the jerk." Brett grimaced. She wouldn't have if he'd stayed around.

But you didn't. You left her alone and pregnant.

That realization made him feel like a heel. While Willow had been raising their little boy, he'd been sleeping around and smiling at cameras.

It was a wonder she didn't hate him.

"Hoberman will let me know if they turn up anything else useful. But finding those prints is enough to obtain a warrant for the men. I need Howard's body, though."

Brett stood and pushed his chair back. "All right, I'll show you where he is." He poked his head in the kitchen and called Mama Mary's name. "I have to go with Maddox. Will you take care of Sam this morning?"

"Of course. Rose is here, too. She loves kids and Sam knows her from when Willow stopped in at her store."

"Tell her I said thanks. We'll be back in a bit."

He grabbed his jacket and followed Maddox to his SUV.

"I wish you'd come to me before," Maddox said.

Brett winced as his stitches pulled. "I'm sorry, Maddox. I didn't want to put you on the spot."

"Didn't want to put me on the spot?" Maddox

said gruffly. "You don't think burying a body and covering up a crime put me on the spot?"

"I know it did," Brett said. "But I couldn't let anything happen to Sam."

Maddox cut his look toward him. "Did you know he was yours?"

Pain rocked through Brett. "Not until we rescued him, and I saw him for myself."

Maddox mumbled something low beneath his breath. "He is definitely yours," he finally said with a small smile.

Pride ballooned in Brett's chest. "He is, isn't he?"

A silent understanding passed between them. Sam would be raised a McCullen from now on.

"Where is the grave?" Maddox asked.

Brett pointed to the east and gave him exact directions. Maddox had the ME and Hoberman waiting to meet them, and a few minutes later, Brett walked the ground and showed him the grave.

The CSI team began to dig, turning the damp earth, and Brett checked his watch.

He had less than twenty-four hours now to save Willow.

WILLOW'S SHOULDERS AND FINGERS ached from twisting and turning, and fresh tears of frustration threatened. She couldn't work the damn knot free.

The door opened again, and the thinner of the men appeared with a plate of scrambled eggs on it. He set a bottle of water beside it.

"I have to go to the bathroom," Willow said. Maybe there would be something in the bathroom she could use as a weapon.

He cursed, but gave a little nod, then jerked her up from the bed. "I can't walk," Willow said. "Please untie me so I can use the bathroom and eat."

His beady eyes met hers. "If you try to run, we'll kill you."

Fear nearly choked her, but she whispered that she understood. "I won't run. Brett will get you the money. I know he will."

"He'd better. We're out of patience."

He removed a knife from his pocket and cut the ropes. She shook her hands free, then wiggled her toes as he untied her feet. He gestured toward the hall, and she ducked in and used the facility, then did a quick desperate search for a razor or pair of scissors. Anything to defend herself.

But the cabinet was empty, the bathroom dingy and old, as if the house had been vacant for a long time.

That would make it harder for Brett to find her. She'd already looked out the window and realized they were off the grid and surrounded by woods.

The man pounded on the door and she opened it, trying to play meek as she glanced to the living area and kitchen. She didn't see the bigger man, so decided that he might be gone.

Getting away from one man would be easier than two.

He grabbed her arm, but she lifted her knee and kicked him in the groin. He doubled over and yelped in pain, and she ran toward the kitchen. She spotted a kitchen knife and grabbed it, then flung open the front door.

Cold wind assaulted her, then a man's fist came toward her face. She tried to scream as the man behind her yanked her hair, but her jaw screamed with pain from the blow the bigger guy had landed.

Another blow to her shoulder blade and she dropped the knife and crumpled, writhing in pain. The bigger guy hauled her up over his shoulder, and the world tilted and spun as he carried her outside.

A second later, he opened the trunk and threw her in. Her head hit something hard, a tire iron maybe, and she saw stars.

"I warned you what would happen if you tried to run," the thinner man snarled.

The trunk door slammed shut, pitching her into darkness. She tried to stay conscious, but nausea flooded her.

The last thing she thought before the car engine started and the car jerked away was that they were going to kill her and bury her just as she'd done Leo.

Except they'd do it out here in the middle of nowhere where no one would ever find her.

Chapter Nineteen

Brett's life flashed behind his eyes as he watched the men digging up Leo Howard's body.

A month ago, *hell*, two weeks ago, he'd been grinning for the cameras, at the height of his career, with his future bright in front of him. His agent had even suggested him for a part in a Western movie.

Now he'd not only discovered he had a son but he'd become an accessory to a murder and might be facing charges of tampering with evidence and covering up a crime.

Instead of riding for a living or starring in a movie, he might soon be sitting in a cell.

The plastic he'd wrapped around Leo came into view as the diggers dumped wet soil beside the grave. One of them paused when his shovel hit something. "He's here."

Brett breathed out in relief. For a fraction of a second, he'd actually been afraid that someone might have discovered Howard's body and moved him.

Maddox angled his head toward him. "You wrapped him in plastic?"

"And a rug." Brett grimaced. "I tried to preserve him as best I could."

Maddox motioned for the men to continue while he stepped aside. "Tell me exactly how you found him."

Brett inhaled sharply. "I can do better. I took a picture," Brett said. "I was planning to tell you everything once Sam was safe."

Maddox muttered a low sound. "All right. Let's see."

Brett pulled his phone from his pocket and accessed the picture. "Willow said Howard picked Sam up from a neighbor's then brought him home. We think the men must have been following him or watching the house, and confronted him about the money. When he refused to give it up, they shot him in the chest and took Sam."

Maddox studied the picture. "I'll have forensics process his body and compare evidence from the house to corroborate her story." His brows furrowed. "Did Howard have visitation with Sam?"

"I don't think so. Willow said he didn't want to be a father." Maybe because he'd known Sam wasn't his. Had Howard resented that fact? Had he taken his temper out on Sam?

"Then why did Leo pick Sam up and take him back to the house?"

Brett stewed over that. "Maybe he knew his partners were after him, and he intended to use Sam as leverage."

The breeze picked up dead leaves and dirt, scattering them at his feet. Brett rubbed his hands together against the chilly wind.

"What did Sam tell you about that night?" Maddox asked.

Brett swallowed hard. "Nothing. I…didn't ask him about it. I figured he'd been through enough."

The diggers had uncovered the length of Howard's body along with the bag of bedding. Two of the men climbed in the grave to hoist him from the hole where they'd laid him in the ground.

"I understand why you don't want to upset Sam, but he might have seen where Howard stashed that cash."

Brett's pulse pounded. He hated to make Sam relive that horrible day.

But if he'd seen where Leo hid the cash, he had to talk to him.

Willow's life depended on it.

CLAUSTROPHOBIA THREATENED TO completely panic Willow. She was suffocating in the trunk of this car.

The constant rumbling and bumping over

rocky roads intensified her headache and made her nauseous.

She reminded herself to breathe in and out and remain calm. Brett would bring the money and rescue her. And if he didn't…he'd take care of Sam.

The car finally jerked to a stop, brakes squealing. The sudden change in movement propelled her across the car trunk, and she rolled into the side. Doors slammed.

The men were getting out.

Terrified they'd carried her someplace in the wilderness to kill her and leave her body, she frantically ran her bound hands across the interior of the trunk. It was so dark, she couldn't see, but there had to be a release lever inside.

Although with her hands and feet tied, how in the world would she escape?

A noise sounded, then voices. "What are we going to do with her?"

"Get rid of her."

The female again. And she sounded so cold-hearted.

"We need the money first."

"All right. Then do it. And kill that cowboy, too."

Willow's stomach knotted. Who was that woman?

Doris, Leo's former girlfriend? Or Eleanor, his

grandmother's nurse? Maybe she'd lied and she had been involved with Leo.

"What should we do with the bodies?" one of the men asked.

"There's an old mine near here," the woman said. "Dump their bodies in there, then close up the opening so no one will ever find them."

Tears blurred Willow's eyes. If they killed her and Brett, what would happen to Sam?

BRETT WATCHED AS the medical examiner, a young woman named Dr. Lail, knelt beside Howard's body. One of the crime workers photographed the way he was wrapped in plastic and the rug, then folded those back so she could examine the body.

Brett ignored the pinch of guilt he felt over burying the man in the cold ground. Howard hadn't deserved any better.

"I'll do an autopsy," Dr. Lail said. "But judging from the gunshots, he probably bled out."

Maddox thanked her and supervised while they carried Howard's body to the ME's van to be transported to the morgue.

"We have to notify next of kin. Did he have relatives?" Maddox asked Brett.

"Father and grandmother." Brett gave him their names and addresses.

"I'll ask Deputy Whitefeather to make the notification."

"I need to go to the bank," Brett said. "Then

I'll have a talk with Sam." A talk he dreaded, but one that needed to happen.

Maddox gave a clipped nod. "Call me when you hear from the kidnappers. You aren't meeting them alone."

Worry nagged at Brett. "Maddox, if you come with me, they'll kill her."

Maddox stepped closer to him. "You can't afford not to have my help." Maddox lowered his voice. "Trust me for once, little brother. They won't know I'm there. But you could be walking into a trap. What would happen to Sam if you and Willow both got killed?"

A sick knot thickened Brett's throat. But his answer was immediate. "I'd want you and Rose to raise Sam."

Maddox's gaze met his, a sea of emotions in his eyes. "Of course I would raise him, he's a McCullen, but we aren't going to let anything happen, Brett. Not if we work together."

It had been a long time since they'd worked together on anything. But Sam and Willow were more important than any petty problem they'd had between them.

So he followed Maddox to the SUV, and they drove into town. Brett went in the bank while Maddox walked across the street to the jail to talk to his deputy about making the death notification.

Brett spotted his business manager, Frank Cotton, waiting in a chair outside the bank president's office. Cotton stood and greeted him with a worried expression, one hand clutching a leather bag.

"Are you going to tell me what this is about now?" Cotton asked worriedly.

Brett motioned for him to keep quiet and they moved against the wall. "I'm sorry, but I can't."

Cotton tugged at his tie. "Listen, if you're in trouble with one of those rodeo groupies, just tell me and I'll make it go away."

Brett jerked his head back. "What are you suggesting?"

"I'm here to do whatever you need, Brett. If you want a girl run off, I'm your man. If you need a lawyer to, say…draw up a confidentiality agreement or adoption papers for a kid, or pay for an abortion, I'll handle it. We won't let anything stand in the way of your career."

Brett stared at him, disturbed by the offer. At one time, his career had been all that mattered. But now he didn't give a damn about it.

All that mattered was Willow and Sam.

And he'd just reconnected with Maddox. Granted they still had things to work out— whether or not Maddox would arrest him—but he wanted to be part of Maddox's life.

And part of Horseshoe Creek.

"Thanks," he told Cotton. "But I'm not paying off a girl. If I need a lawyer, I'll let you know."

He took the leather bag, then glimpsed inside. Cash, just as he'd requested. "Just keep this between us, Cotton."

"Of course."

Brett turned to leave. "Your agent's been calling," Cotton said. "She wants to talk about your schedule this spring."

"I'll get in touch with her," Brett said.

He stepped outside the bank and started to cross the street, but a truck whizzed by and he jumped back as a bullet flew toward him.

Chapter Twenty

Brett ducked behind a pole, just as another bullet whizzed by his head. Who was shooting at him?

He tried to get a look at the driver, but the truck roared down the road in a cloud of exhaust. Then someone slammed something hard against the back of his head, and he stumbled and went down. He tried to hold on to the bag of cash, but someone snatched it from his hands and raced away.

"Everyone get down!" Maddox yelled as he jogged from across the street, his gun drawn, his gaze sweeping the area for the shooter.

A few locals on the street screamed and darted in different directions. Brett pushed to his hands and stood, cursing as he hunted for the person who'd just stolen the cash. But he'd come out of nowhere and disappeared just as quickly.

Maddox was breathing hard, his gaze still surveying the street as he approached Brett. "Are you hit?"

"No. The shooter drove off, but another guy punched me and stole the money."

Maddox pivoted again. "The shooter was a decoy meant to distract you so the other man could sneak up behind."

"Yeah, and he succeeded."

"Did you get a look at either one of them?"

"No, not really. The license plate on the truck was missing. The one who took the money was big and wore a hoodie."

Brett's manager stepped from the bank, looking terrified. "Brett, man, are you all right?"

"Yeah, but he stole the money." Brett scraped his hand through his hair, frustrated. "I can't believe this is happening."

Maddox narrowed his eyes at the manager. "Did you see anything?"

The tall man fiddled with his bolo tie. "No, I heard the gunshot, and like everyone in the bank, we dropped to the floor and hid. We thought someone was coming in to rob the bank."

"It had to be the bastards who have Willow," Brett said. "They must have followed me here, and decided to take the cash and run."

His heart stuttered. Which meant that they might have given up on the other money and killed Willow.

AN HOUR LATER, Brett entered the farmhouse. Anxiety churned in his gut. Maddox had canvassed everyone in the bank, the street and business owners, but no one had seen anything.

Once the first shot had rent the air, panic had set in. It was a small town. The locals weren't used to high crime or random attacks...or murder.

But they would know soon enough that a kidnapping had occurred and that a man had been shot to death right here in their safe little town.

Rose greeted Maddox with a big hug and kiss. If Brett hadn't been so fraught with fear for Willow, he would have laughed at the mushy look on his big brother's face as he locked lips with her.

Sam raced in from the kitchen. "Did you get Mommy back?"

Brett's lungs squeezed for air. He'd never look at life the same way now that he had a little boy.

Maddox, Rose and Mama Mary gave him sympathetic looks.

"We were making cookies to surprise her when she comes home," Mama Mary said, wiping flour from Sam's cheek with a gentle hand.

"And Sam made her a card," Rose added with a smile.

Brett stooped down to Sam's level. "She's not with me now, but we're going to find her, little man. And she's going to love the cookies and card."

Sam's face fell into a pout. "We're making peanut butter. That's Mommy's favorite."

Emotions nearly choked Brett. He remembered

that about Willow. One time she'd eaten half a dozen of Mama Mary's famous peanut butter cookies. He clasped Sam's hand in his. "Come in here with me a minute, bud. I need to talk to you."

Sam clamped his teeth over his lip, but followed him to the den. Brett wanted to wrap his arms around his son and swear to him that everything would be all right.

But he had to find Sam's mother first or he would be making empty promises.

"Sam, I'm trying to figure out where those bad men are keeping your mommy. Do you remember anything else about the place?"

"No. Just that it was dark, and it smelled bad." The little boy dropped his head and picked at the button on Brett's shirt.

"How about your daddy? What can you tell me about him?"

Sam turned his face up toward Brett. "He was mean to Mommy and he didn't want me."

The breath left Brett's lungs in a rush. He lifted Sam's chin with his thumb. He wanted to assure him that he wanted him, but that would take an explanation he didn't have time for right now. But it would happen. "You know, that's not your fault. You are a wonderful kid."

Sam simply stared at him with big frightened eyes. "Daddy didn't think so. He said I was a baby, and I was in the way."

Brett wrapped his arm around his son. He wished Leo was alive so he could kill him. "That's not true, Sam. You're very special and your mommy loves you with all her heart." *And so do I.* "I care about you, too."

Sam looked up at him. "I see why my mommy liked you when she was in school. You're nicer than Daddy. He yelled at Mommy all the time."

"That's because he was a bad man."

Sam looked down again. "But if he was bad and the other men killed him, why did they take me and Mommy?"

"Because your daddy stole money from them, and they're greedy and want it back."

"There was lots of it?" Sam said.

"Yes." Brett rubbed Sam's back. "Did you see your daddy with any money?"

He shook his head.

Brett hesitated, trying to word his questions carefully. "Daddy picked you up at your mommy's friend's house that day?"

"Yeah. I didn't wanna go with him, but Miss Gina said I should."

Brett chewed the inside of his cheek. "What happened when you and Leo got back to your house?"

Sam kept tugging at Brett's button, his little body trembling slightly. Brett rubbed Sam's back. "I know it's hard to think about, but buddy, it might help."

A long moment lapsed between them, then Sam's breath wheezed out. "We went inside, and he tolded me to hide in my room."

"What? Why?"

"He said some men followed him."

So Leo had tried to protect Sam. That was something.

"Did he have anything with him?"

Sam scrunched his nose. "Like what?"

"Maybe a briefcase or suitcase."

Sam's eyes lit up. "He gots a big gym bag and brought it in the house. Then he pushed me in the closet and shut the door and told me not to come out."

"You stayed in the closet?"

Sam nodded. "I was scared. I just wanted Daddy to go away. But he said he had to get some stuff he left with Mommy."

"Did she say what stuff?"

"No, and Mommy said she threw the stuff he left away. But he said he hid it there. I was scared he'd get mad about that, so I didn't tell him."

Smart boy.

"After you got in the closet, what did your father do?"

Sam's finger twisted the button harder. "He took my toys out of my toy box and throwed them on the floor."

Brett imagined the scene, questions ticking in his head. He and Willow had searched the house, but what if Leo had stowed the money in that toy chest?

"Then someone busted in. I heard the door cracking, then those awful men shouting and Daddy gots up and tried to talk to them."

Brett cradled Sam in his arms, holding him tight.

"They yelled and said ugly words, then Daddy jumped on one of them and...the gun went off."

His heart ached for his little boy. To witness a murder at such a young age was bound to affect him, maybe give him nightmares. Possibly for years to come.

He needed his mother to help him through the trauma.

He also needed a father.

"I'm sorry you had to see that, Sam, but you're very brave to tell me about it." Sam shivered, and Brett hugged him with all the love in his heart.

Then he cupped Sam's face in his hands. "I need you to be strong just a little while longer, okay?"

Sam nodded, the trust in his son's look nearly bringing Brett to his knees.

WILLOW'S BODY ACHED from being tied up and bound in the trunk of the car. She was suffocating.

But they didn't seem to be in a hurry to let her

out. In fact, it had gotten quiet for a while and she thought they might have left her.

The sound of another engine roaring rent the air. Tires screeched. Then more doors slammed.

"Where have you two been?" the woman asked.

"We got that money McCullen promised."

"He found Leo's stash?" the woman asked.

"No, the money McCullen withdrew from his own funds. With that and Leo's money, we'll all be set for a long time."

"You idiot," the woman said. "He's liable to call the cops."

"And tell them what?" the man barked. "That someone stole ransom money? That he buried Leo's body? I doubt that rodeo star wants that in the papers."

"It's time for us to make the meet," the other man said. "If McCullen doesn't bring the cash Leo stole this time, let's get rid of the woman and get out of town before things heat up.

The trunk opened, and Willow clenched her teeth as the bigger guy hauled her to the ground. She stumbled, then gasped when she saw the woman.

Gina, her neighbor. The woman she'd thought was her friend.

Dear God... "Why?"

Gina gave her a nasty grin. "Because Leo was

supposed to be mine. And so was this money. And with you out of the way, now it will be."

The big guy, Norman she'd heard him called, punched a number on his cell phone. It must be Wally Norman. A minute later, she heard Brett's voice.

"Hello. This is Brett McCullen."

"I'm texting you an address. If you want to see the woman again, bring the cash and come alone."

"Let me speak to Willow first," Brett said.

Willow shuddered as the big guy pressed a gun to her temple. "Say hello, honey."

"Brett, I'm okay, just take care of Sam!"

The man jerked the phone away, then whacked her on the back of the head again and shoved her back in the trunk.

Tears caught in her throat. The drop-off was a trap.

Chapter Twenty-One

Brett left Sam to finish the cookies and card with Mama Mary and motioned for Maddox to join him in the hall. "Maddox, I received a text about the drop."

"Where?"

Brett angled the phone for Maddox to see the address. "Do you know where that is?"

Maddox shrugged. "Yeah. It's not too far from here."

"I also may know where the stolen money is."

"Where?"

"Sam said that when Leo picked him up, he had a bag with him, and that he was digging around in Sam's toy chest."

"Did you look there before?"

"I saw the chest but all that was visible was toys. Maybe he hid it under them."

"Let's go." Maddox grabbed his keys, but Brett put a hand to his brother's shoulder.

"Not in your SUV, Maddox. If they see you, they'll kill Willow."

Maddox exhaled. "You're right. We'll drive your truck."

Seconds later, they raced to Willow's house. Crime-scene tape marked the house and fingerprint dust coated everything inside.

Worse, the house smelled of death and emptiness, not like a home, but like a place where a terrible wrong had been done. Would Willow want to return here?

"The toy chest?" Maddox asked, jarring him back to the moment.

Brett pushed all thoughts aside and hurried into Sam's room. Knowing Sam was his son made the toys and posters on the wall seem more personal and they tugged at his heart.

Toys had been dumped and scattered across the floor from the toy chest. A football, toy trucks, plastic horses, a plastic bat and ball.

"You see it?" Maddox asked behind him.

"No." He quickly emptied the remaining toys, then felt along the bottom and discovered a piece of plywood. Had that board come with the toy chest?

A nail felt loose, and he pulled at it until the board loosened, then he yanked it free. "I found it!" Cash was neatly stacked and spread evenly across the bottom.

Maddox handed him the duffel bag, and Brett quickly filled it with the money.

Nerves tightened his neck and Brett watched for another ambush as he carried it out to his truck. Seconds later, Brett sped from the house.

"Listen, Brett, when we get there, I'll stay down until we see what we're dealing with."

Maddox checked his gun, and Brett grimaced. His rifle lay on the seat between them. If he needed it, he'd use it in a heartbeat.

Dark clouds rolled overhead, the wind picking up as he turned down the road into the woods. Trees shook and limbs swayed as he neared the cabin, and he searched for signs that Willow was there.

"What do you see?"

Brett squinted through the dark. "An old cabin, looks like it's been deserted for a while. I don't see anyone. One light on in the house from a back room."

"How about a vehicle?"

"A dark sedan. Tinted windows. I can't see if anyone is inside."

"Park and sit there for a minute. Wait and see if anyone comes outside."

Brett did as he said, his senses alert as he scanned the exterior of the cabin. An old weathered building sat to the right. It appeared empty, but someone could be hiding inside.

A sound to the left made him jerk his head

to see what it was. A deer scampered through the woods.

He hissed a breath, then reached for the door handle. "It's time. I have to see if she's here."

Maddox caught his arm and looked up at him from the floorboard of the truck. "Be careful, Brett. This could be a setup."

He knew that.

But he had to take that chance.

He eased open the door and slid one foot from the truck. Clutching the duffel bag with the other hand, he lowered himself to the ground. He visually surveyed the area again, his stitches tugging as he slowly walked toward the cabin.

"I've got your money," he shouted.

The front door to the cabin opened, and he braced himself for gunfire. If they killed him, at least Maddox was armed and could save Willow and take her home to Sam.

WILLOW FELT DIZZY from being locked in the trunk of the car and inhaling the exhaust as they'd driven.

The car jerked to a stop, and she forced tears at bay. Crying would do no good. These people didn't care about her.

All they wanted was money.

The trunk opened, and she squinted, blinded by the sudden light. Then a cold hard hand clamped around her wrist and dragged her from the car again. She stumbled, dizzy and disoriented.

"Day should be meeting with McCullen now," the man named Norman said.

Gina gestured to the right. Willow looked around, sick when she realized that they were in the middle of nowhere.

And that Gina was pointing to an old mine. Rusted mining equipment sat discarded, piles of dirt scattered around along with metal garbage cans and tools.

"How can you do this, Gina? Sam is just an innocent little boy. He needs me."

"He'll survive," Gina said.

"Did you kill Leo?" Willow asked.

"He deserved it. He tried to betray me, just like he did Norman and Day."

"Why did Leo take Sam to my house?" Willow asked. "Why didn't he just get the money and leave?"

Gina hissed. "He knew Norman broke out of jail, and he and Day were onto him."

Hate swelled inside Willow. Leo had taken Sam with him as insurance.

"And you followed him to my house and killed him," Willow said, piecing together the most logical scenario.

"No, that was Norman," Gina said. "He said Leo attacked him."

"So when he died that day, you kidnapped Sam?"

"We earned that money the hard way." Gina waved a hand toward the mine. "And when Jasper gets back with it, we'll flee the country and live the good life."

Panic clawed at Willow. Norman reached for her and she tried to run, but with her ankles bound together, it was futile. She stumbled, then he threw her over his shoulder like a sack of potatoes and carted her toward the mine.

BRETT PAUSED AT the foot of the steps. A thin man with a goatee and tattoos on his neck appeared, a .38 pointed at Brett. Jasper Day.

"Toss the money on the porch," Day ordered. "And you'd better not try to cheat us this time."

"You're the crook and the murderer, not me."

Day's laugh boomeranged through the silence as he waved the gun. "Throw it now."

Brett clenched the bag tighter. "First, I want to see Willow."

Day shook his head. "Not going to happen. I'm calling the shots here."

Brett had a bad feeling this was going south. That Willow wasn't here. If she was dead…

"Either you bring her out here, or I walk back to the truck."

Day cursed. "You're a fool. I've got a gun

pointed at your head, and you think you can bluff your way out of this."

"I don't care about the money," Brett shouted, "but I'll give my life for Willow. Now show me that she's alive."

Day's hand shook as he took a menacing step toward Brett. "Put the bag down now, McCullen. This isn't one of your rodeo games."

Brett held his ground and yelled for Willow. "Is she in there?" He gestured toward the cabin, and Day glanced sideways with a cocky grin.

Brett took advantage of that small sideways look, swung the bag and threw it with all his might. The bag slammed into Day with such force that it threw him backward. But he managed to get off a shot before he fell.

Brett dodged the bullet, then Maddox jumped from the truck and fired at Day. One bullet into Day's chest, and he crumpled to the ground with a bellow. His gun skittered to the ground beside him as the man's arm fell limp.

Brett and Maddox ran toward him, then Maddox kicked the gun away, knelt beside the bastard and handcuffed him to the porch rail. Brett started toward the house, but Maddox called his name. He was right behind him, holding Day's gun. "Take this."

Brett snatched Day's revolver and inched up to the house. Maddox motioned for him to let him enter first, and Maddox eased through the door.

He glanced in all directions, then gestured for Brett to go right and he'd go left.

Brett gripped the weapon with sweaty hands and inched across the wood floor. A bedroom to the right made his heart stop. A single metal bed sat by the wall, ropes discarded on the floor, a food tray, a ratty stuffed animal…

This was where they'd held his son. And they'd probably brought Willow to the same room.

But no one was inside now. He looked for blood but didn't see any. That had to be a good sign, didn't it?

He stepped into the hall and found Maddox frowning. "There's no one here, Brett."

Fear knotted his insides. "Where is she, Maddox?"

"Let's ask Day. He'll know." Brett followed him back outside but Day was barely conscious.

Brett dropped down beside him and snatched the man by the collar. "Where did your partner take Willow?"

The man looked up at him with glazed eyes. "Doctor…" he rasped.

Brett held up his phone. "I'll call for help when you tell me where they took her."

Day spit at him. "Go to hell."

Brett lifted Day's own gun to the criminal's head. "No, that's where you're going if you don't talk."

Chapter Twenty-Two

"You won't do it," Day rasped.

"You're sure about that?" Brett said darkly. "Because that little boy you kidnapped is my son. And his mother means everything to me."

The man's eyes bulged, and he coughed up blood.

Maddox aimed his gun at the other side of Day's head. "Where is she, Day?"

"The old mine off Snakepit Road."

Brett shoved away from the man, sick to his stomach. That mine had been shut down for years. And the road was dubbed Snakepit Road because miners had complained about the hotbed of snakes in the area.

"I have to go," Brett told Maddox.

Maddox looked down at Day. They both knew he wouldn't make it, but could they just leave him?

"Go ahead. I'll call for an ambulance and be right behind you." Maddox caught his arm. "Be careful, little brother. Don't do anything stupid. Wait for me to move in."

Brett muttered that he would, although if he had to go in on his own to save Willow, they both knew he'd do it.

Without Willow and Sam, his life meant nothing.

WILLOW SHIVERED WITH cold and fear as Norman tossed her to the ground inside the mine. She'd grown accustomed to the dark trunk, but this dark cavern wreaked of decayed animals and other foul odors she didn't even want to identify.

Norman cast his flashlight around the hole where he'd put her, and she cringed at the sight of the dirt walls. He must have dragged her a half mile inside. Wooden posts that supported beams inside the mine had been built when the mine was being worked, and Norman dragged her over to one and tied her to the post. Rocks and dirt scraped her arms and jeans, the jagged edges of loose stones cutting into her side.

"I wouldn't fight it too much," he said with an ugly sneer. "These beams are old and rotting. If one comes down, the whole mine may cave in."

"Why are you warning me?" Willow demanded. "You're going to leave me here to die anyway."

His thick brows drew together in a unibrow as he looked down at her. Then he turned and left her without another word. A snake hissed somewhere in the dark, and she pressed herself against the mine wall and pulled her knees up to her chest, trying to make herself as small as possible.

Not that the snake wouldn't find her anyway.

The light faded as Norman disappeared through the mine shaft, and she dropped her head forward, fighting despair.

Brett would have no idea how to find her. She was going to die here in this hellhole, and he would never know how sorry she was that she'd kept Sam from him.

Or that she'd never stopped loving him.

BRETT SCANNED THE DIRT road and deserted mine ahead as he sped down Snakepit Road.

There were no cars, no trucks, nothing to indicate anyone was here.

Fear seized him. Had Day lied to them? Had they taken Willow somewhere else?

His tires screeched as he barreled past the sign that marked the mine and threw the truck in Park. He jumped out, shouting Willow's name as he ran toward the opening of the mine, but just as he neared it, he noticed dynamite attached to the door and some kind of trigger, as if it was set with a timer.

Terror clawed at him, and he rushed to tear the dynamite away, but he was too late. The explosion sent him flying backward against some rocks, the sound of the mine collapsing roaring in his ears.

For a moment, he was so disoriented he couldn't breathe. Dust blurred his vision. His ears rang.

But fear and reality seeped through the haze. Was Willow inside that mine? Was he too late to save her?

He shoved himself up from the ground, raking dirt and twigs from his hair and clothes as he raced back toward the opening. "Willow! Willow, are you in there?!"

He dropped to his knees and started to yank boards away, but when he did, all he found was dirt. Mounds and mounds of it…

She might be buried alive in there…

Tears clogged his eyes and throat, and he bellowed in despair. But he lurched to his feet, ran to his truck, grabbed his cell phone and punched Maddox's number.

"I'm on my way, Brett."

"Get help!" Brett shouted. "They're gone, but there was dynamite outside the opening of the mine and it just exploded. I think Willow's inside."

A tense moment passed, then Maddox's breath rattled over the line. "I'll call a rescue crew and an ambulance," Maddox said. "Just hang in there, man."

Brett jammed the phone in his pocket and ran

back toward the mine, yelling Willow's name over and over and praying she could hear.

It seemed like hours later that Maddox arrived. His brother Ray shocked him by showing up on his heels. "Just tell me what to do," Ray said, his dark eyes fierce.

"We have to get her out," Brett said. "She has to be alive."

"A crew is on its way with equipment," Maddox said. "We need an engineer, someone who knows the mine, Brett, or we could make things worse."

How in the hell could they get worse? Willow was trapped, probably fighting for her life.

Ray cleared his throat. "Let me take a look. Maybe there's another entrance. Another way inside."

Ray's calm voice offered Brett a glimmer of hope, and he followed his younger brother, hoping he was right. They walked the edge of the mine shaft following it for half a mile, searching brush and rock structures for a second entrance.

"There had to be an extra exit for safety," Ray said.

He walked ahead, climbing a hill, then disappeared down an embankment. Brett was just about to give up when Ray shouted his name. "Over here. I found it!"

He looked up and saw Ray waving him forward. The sound of trucks barreling down the graveled road rent the air, and he looked back to Maddox who was waving the rescue crew toward the site.

"I'll tell Maddox I'm going in this end and check it out," Ray said.

Brett nodded and waited until Ray went down the hill, then he dropped to his stomach and crawled inside.

He couldn't wait. Every second that passed meant Willow was losing oxygen and might die.

The mine shaft was so low at the exit that he had to slide in on his belly. He used his pocket flashlight to light the way and slithered on his stomach, dragging himself through the narrow tunnel until he reached a taller section that had been carved under rock. It was a room with supports built, giving him enough room to stand up.

"Willow! Can you hear me?"

He waved the light around the tunnel, searching for other crawl spaces, and spotted one to the left. He dropped down again, ignoring the dust and pebbles raining down on him, well aware the whole damn thing could collapse in seconds.

"Willow!" He continued to yell her name and search until finally he heard a sound.

"Willow, can you hear me? If you can, make some noise!"

Please let her be alive.

He crawled a few more feet, then reached another clearing where more supports indicated another room, although it appeared the roof had collapsed in the center. Willow must be on the other side. "Willow!"

"Brett!"

He breathed out in relief. "Hang in there, honey, I'm coming."

He started to dig with his hands, but realized tools would make the process faster, so he crawled back the way he came. It seemed to take him forever to reach the exit. He sucked in fresh air as he crawled out and raced down the hill to where the other men were starting to get set up.

"I told you to wait," Ray said.

Brett blew off his concern. "I found her. But I need a shovel or pick to dig her out."

"We've got this, Mr. McCullen," one of the rescue workers said. "It's too dangerous for you."

Why? Because he was a damn celebrity. "I don't care. I have to save her."

"They're the experts." Ray stepped up beside him. "One wrong move in there, Brett, and you could bring the whole mine down."

Maddox placed a hand on his back. "Brett, let them do their jobs. Besides, it won't help Sam if you get yourself killed."

"Who's Sam?" Ray asked.

Brett rubbed a hand down his face and began to explain to his younger brother that he had a son.

WILLOW FADED IN and out of consciousness. She couldn't breathe, couldn't find the air.

What had happened? One minute she'd been tied down here, praying Brett would find her. Then…something had exploded.

The roof had come tumbling down, rocks and dirt pummeling her. She'd tried to cover her face and head, but it had happened so quickly, and now dirt and rocks covered her. She tried to move her legs but they wouldn't budge.

Either she was paralyzed or the weight of the dirt was too heavy…

Her head lolled to the side, and she forced herself to inhale shallow breaths to conserve air. She thought she'd heard Brett calling her name.

Or had she been hallucinating because she was so close to death?

She closed her eyes and tried to envision someone rescuing her. Pictured Brett carrying her to safety and fresh air. Saw the two of them walking with Sam in the pasture, sharing a picnic, then telling Sam that Brett was his father.

Next, Brett was proposing, promising her they'd be the family they should have been all along.

The earth rumbled, some loud noise sounded and the mine began to tremble and shake again. She closed her eyes and mouth against another onslaught of debris, but when she opened them, her head was almost completely covered, and she choked on the dirt.

WITH EVERY SECOND that ticked by, Brett thought he was going to die himself. Maddox let the rescue crew take charge of finding Willow, while he issued an APB for Wally Norman. Authorities were alerted at airports, train and bus stations, and the police in states bordering Wyoming. He even notified border patrol in Mexico and Canada, although they didn't intend to let Norman get that far. Tire marks indicated that he'd been driving a sedan, although he could ditch that anywhere. *Hell*, he could have changed vehicles already and picked up a disguise.

"We're almost through!" one of the men shouted. They'd set up a man on the outside with receivers to communicate, as the two other rescue workers crawled inside.

Brett paced by the exit, grateful when an ambulance arrived.

"I can't believe you have a kid," Ray said.

"Me either." And he'd almost lost him and Willow.

But he was grateful Maddox and Ray were here. They hadn't exactly spent any time together since he'd returned. The three of them had retreated to their separate corners, just as they had as kids.

Except now Maddox had put his job on the line

for him. And Ray…well, he'd come to his aid, no questions asked.

"They've got her!" one of the men shouted.

Brett rushed to the outside of the exit, desperate to see Willow. Ray stood behind him, silent but strong, as if he'd be there to catch him if he fell apart. It was an odd feeling, one he hadn't had in a long time.

Everyone in his business and the rodeo wanted something from him, wanted to build off his fame, wanted his money, wanted a part of him. But his brothers were here, just to support him.

Their father would have been proud.

Another agonizing few minutes stretched by, but finally one of the men slowly emerged, dragging a board through the opening.

A board with Willow strapped to it.

She was so filthy and covered in dirt and bruises that he could hardly see her face.

He held his breath as he dropped to her side and raked her hair back from her cheek. Her eyes were closed, and she lay terrifyingly still. "Willow?"

He looked up at the rescue worker, desperate for good news.

The man looked worried, his expression bleak as his partner emerged from the mine.

Brett cradled Willow's hand in his as the men lifted the board to carry her to the ambulance.

"Get the paramedics!" one of the rescue workers yelled.

More shouts and two medics ran toward them.

Brett whispered Willow's name again. "Wil-
low, please wake up, baby. Sam and I need you."
Suddenly he felt a tiny something in his hand.
Willow's fingers twitching, grasping for him.

Brett choked on tears as she finally opened her
eyes and looked at him.

THE NEXT TWO HOURS were chaos. Brett rode with
the ambulance to the hospital, whispering promises to Willow that he wouldn't leave her side. She
was weak and had suffered bruises and contu-
sions and possibly a concussion. She also needed
oxygen and rest.

"Gina," she whispered. "My friend."

"What? You want me to call her?"

"No. She was in on it," Willow rasped. "She
was helping Leo. She told Norman to kill me."

"I'll tell Maddox to issue an APB for her, too."

She broke into a coughing spell, and he helped
her sip some water. "Sam."

"He's home with Mama Mary," Brett said. "I
called and told them you're all right. I'll bring
Sam to visit tomorrow."

Willow clung to his hand. "No, I'll go home
and be with him." A tear slid down her cheek.
"Only I don't know where home is. I can't go
back to that house where Leo was killed."

"Shh." Brett stroked her cheek. "Don't worry about anything tonight, Willow."

She breathed heavily, then looked up at him again. "About Sam, Brett..."

"I told you not to worry about anything," he whispered. "We'll find a way to work it out."

Although, as she faded into sleep again, Brett laid his head against the edge of the bed and clung to her hand. She had kept Sam from him once and bitterness still gnawed at him for what he'd missed.

Still...he loved Willow and wanted to be a father to his son.

But would Willow want him now after he'd let her down all those years ago?

Chapter Twenty-Three

Willow lapsed in and out of consciousness all night. She dreamt she was dying and that Brett saved her. She dreamt that he left her and walked away and was marrying someone else.

Every time she looked up, though, Brett was there. He stayed by her bed holding her hand and reassuring her she was all right. He fell asleep in the chair. He gave her water when she was thirsty and wiped her forehead with a cool cloth and held her when she woke screaming that she was drowning in dirt.

But sometime in the early morning, she stirred and heard him on the phone.

"Yes, Ginger, I know the movie offer is a big deal." Pause. "I realize it's a cowboy part, that it would take me to a new level."

Willow closed her eyes, her heart aching. Brett was already planning to leave her just as he had before. Except this time when he left, he would know he had a son.

She steeled herself to accept his decision. She would no more trap him now than she had five years ago.

And she'd never let him see how much he'd hurt her.

BRETT HAD NEVER prayed so much in his damn life.

Even when they'd finally moved Willow from the ER into a room, he'd been terrified she'd stop breathing.

Her screams of terror had wrenched his heart.

The nurse checked her vitals, the doctor appeared to examine her and Brett stepped out to call home. Maddox answered on the first ring.

"How is she?"

"All right. How's Sam?"

"Asking about her, but Mama Mary and Rose are feeding him funny-face pancakes and he's gobbling them up."

Brett had always loved Mama Mary's funny-face pancakes. Especially the chocolate-chip eyes.

"There's more. We caught Norman and Gina. They're being transported back here to face charges."

"Thank God." He swallowed hard. "What about me and Willow?"

"I explained everything to the local judge. And this morning I arrested Boyle Gates. Seems Day spilled Gates's involvement and the way they framed Garcia. Gus is going to be released. I offered him a job here on the ranch, so he and his wife and daughter can have a fresh start."

"You've been busy."

"I just like to see justice done. And Garcia needs a second chance."

Maddox was a stand-up guy. "Dad would be proud of you."

"He'd be proud of you, too, little brother."

"I don't know about that. Willow would never have gotten in this mess if I'd stuck around."

A second passed. "Maybe not. But that was then. What are you going to do *now*?"

Brett glanced back at the hospital room. "I'm going to fix things, if I can."

He ended the call and went in to see Willow. She was sitting up in bed, but her expression was guarded, her eyes flat.

"How are you feeling?"

"I need to go home and be with Sam."

"I'll tell Mama Mary to bring you some clothes and if the doctor releases you, I'll drive you back to the cabin."

Willow shook her head. "I can't go back there, Brett. Not with you." She hesitated and averted her eyes. "Our time has passed."

Brett's lungs squeezed for air. She wasn't even going to give him a chance?

He couldn't accept that. "Willow, you've been

through a terrible ordeal. We all have. I was terrified that I'd lost you. Maybe you blame me for that, for everything."

She slipped from bed, hugging the hospital gown around her. "Don't, Brett. I'd appreciate it if you'd ask Mama Mary or Rose to bring me some clothes so I can shower and get Sam. Then we'll find a place to stay on our own."

Brett watched with a hollow feeling in his gut as she stepped into the bathroom and shut the door.

He phoned Mama Mary, and she agreed to bring Sam and some clothes. Willow must have gotten soap and shampoo from the nurse. By the time she was finished showering in the bathroom and in a clean hospital gown, Mama Mary was there.

She knocked and peeked in the door with a smile. When Willow saw Sam, her face lit up. She opened her arms and he fell into them.

The two of them hugged like they hadn't seen each other for years.

Suddenly Brett felt like the outsider. Like an intruder who didn't belong.

He stepped outside to gather his composure, his emotions in a tailspin. He'd thought he and Willow had gotten close again, that she had feelings for him. But had he hurt her too much for her to forgive him? Didn't she want him to be part of Sam's life?

Mama Mary patted his shoulder. "I'm sorry, son. But Willow asked me to drive her to a hotel. I don't understand what's going on between you two, but she probably just needs some time."

Or maybe he'd lost his chance years ago and Willow would never love him again.

THREE DAYS LATER, Willow was still miserable. She and Sam were temporarily staying in a small apartment above the fabric store in town. The lady who commissioned several of her quilts had been generous, and Willow had jumped at the chance to be close to town. Somehow she felt safer knowing the sheriff's office was down the street.

But she missed Brett, and so did Sam.

She pushed the boxes of pictures that she'd brought with her into the closet. *Out of sight, out of mind.*

Except she couldn't get Brett out of her mind. Which made her furious at herself.

Brett was probably packing to leave for his big movie role. Planning a hot, sexy, wild night with that woman, Ginger.

She would be only a whisper of a memory to him once he got to Hollywood and the sophisticated women who were probably dying to have a cowboy in their bed swarmed after him.

Sam lined his toy ponies on the floor, then

pretended to gallop them around the pasture. How could she not look at her son and see Brett?

Worse, she didn't know what to say to Sam. How to explain why they weren't staying at the ranch anymore.

They still hadn't told Sam that Brett was his father. Brett hadn't pushed either.

Maybe he wanted it that way. If that was the case, it was best that Sam stay in the dark.

Determined to distract herself, she sorted through the mail. A white envelope written in calligraphy caught her eye. She opened the envelope, surprised to find a wedding invitation to Maddox and Rose's wedding.

It was to be a simple affair, just family and a few friends, and would take place at Horseshoe Creek.

She tucked the invitation back in the envelope, her heart aching. She wasn't family, but Sam was. Only he had no idea that he belonged to the McCullens.

Could she deprive him of that?

BRETT HAD TRIED to take Mama Mary's advice and give Willow time. But every day without her and Sam in his life was so painful he could barely breathe.

But today was his brother's wedding, and of course it made him think of Willow and the wedding they'd never had. The one they should have had.

The one he wanted.

But after all Maddox had done for him, he had to put his brother first today.

Chaos filled the house as Mama Mary ushered everyone around. The caterers, florist, the vendor with the tables and tent they'd ordered for the lawn.

And of course, him and Ray.

She'd insisted they wear long duster jackets and bolo ties, since they were standing up for Maddox.

Brett was his best man.

He felt humbled and honored and so damn glad to be home at Horseshoe Creek that he never wanted to leave.

The realization hit him, and he stepped into his old room and called his agent to tell her he was going to refuse the movie deal. He was done putting on shows.

He would stick around here and help Maddox run the ranch. And one day he would win Willow back.

Determination renewed, he left a message for Ginger, then strode down the steps. Maddox looked nervous but happier than any man had a right to be. He'd invited the ranch hands, Gus Garcia and his family, and Deputy Whitefeather, who seemed standoffish to him and Ray, though he didn't have time to contemplate the reason.

The weather had warmed today, a breeze stirring the trees, but the sun was shining, the flowers Rose had chosen dotting the landscape with color.

"Come on, brothers. It's time," Maddox said.

Brett and Ray followed Maddox and found the guests already seated in white chairs by the creek. Mama Mary and Rose had created an altar of flowers between two trees where Rose stood, looking like an angel.

The smile she gave Maddox sparkled with love.

Maddox was a damn lucky man.

Ray fidgeted with his tie, as if it was choking him, but Brett pasted on his camera-ready smile. As he and Ray took their places, he glanced at the guests and saw Willow and Sam sitting by Mama Mary.

His heart nearly stopped. She looked so beautiful in that pale green dress with her long hair billowing around her shoulders. Gone were the bruises and dirt from the mine, although her eyes still held remnants of the horror.

Was she still having those bad dreams? Who was holding her at night and soothing her when she did?

How about Sam? He looked handsome in that Western shirt and bolo tie. It was almost like Brett's. But did he have nightmares at night, too?

He was so enamored with watching the two of them that for a moment the ceremony faded to a blur and he imagined that he and Willow were the ones declaring their love.

Ray poked him. "The ring, brother."

He jolted back to the present and handed Maddox the simple gold band he'd bought for Rose.

Maddox and Rose exchanged vows, then kissed and cheers erupted. He and Ray turned to congratulate them, yet all Brett could do was wish he and Willow were the ones getting married today.

Champagne, whiskey, beer and wine flowed at the reception on the lawn by the creek that the ranch had been named for, and he took a shot of whiskey for courage, then went to talk to Willow before she could run.

He wanted her and Sam, and he didn't intend to back down without a fight.

He found her standing with Sam by the creek. She was trying to teach him how to skip rocks, but she had it all wrong.

He picked up a smooth stone, squeezed Sam's shoulder and then showed him the McCullen way. Willow's gaze met his, sadness and regret flickering in the depths.

But for a brief second, he saw desire spark. Enough desire to warm his heart and give him a second jolt of courage.

Sam squealed when the water rippled at his next attempt, and Brett patted his back. "Good job."

Sam stooped to collect more stones, and Brett brushed Willow's arm. "You look beautiful tonight."

A sweet blush stained her cheeks. "I thought you'd be gone by now," she finally said.

Brett shrugged. "Maybe I don't want to go."

She gestured toward Maddox and Rose who were dancing in the moonlight while the wedding guests watched. "I'm sure Maddox is glad you stayed for the ceremony."

"That's not the reason I stayed."

Sam picked up another stone, raised his hand and sailed it across the creek.

"Good job, Sam."

Sam grinned. "You still gonna let me ride your horses like you promised?"

Willow laid a hand on Sam's shoulder. "Sam, honey, we'll get you lessons somewhere. Brett is a busy man. He has to leave soon. He's going back to the rodeo, and he's going to star in a movie."

Brett's smile faltered. "Where did you get that idea?"

Willow leaned down to speak to Sam for a minute. "If you want a cookie, you can go get one now."

Sam bounced up and down with a grin and ran toward the table with the cookie tray.

"I heard you on the phone with that woman, Ginger. I'm sure she's waiting for you with open arms."

Brett chuckled. Was that a note of jealousy in Willow's voice? "Ginger is my publicist and agent, Willow. Nothing more."

She averted her gaze. "Well, I'm sure there will be lots of women in Hollywood."

"What if I don't want Hollywood?"

"I know you, Brett, you always had big dreams. You belong in the limelight, not here."

Brett squared his shoulders. "You don't want me to be around Sam?"

"That's not what I said."

He cleared his throat, changing the subject. He had to get this out in the open. Had to know the truth. "Why didn't you tell me about him, Willow?"

She closed her eyes for a brief second, her breath unsteady. When she opened them, he saw regret and some other emotion that he couldn't define.

"Why, Willow? Because you didn't think I'd be a good father?"

"*What?* No." Her eyes flared. "You wanted to leave."

"You didn't give me a chance to choose the right thing."

"*The right thing?* What was that, Brett? What was I supposed to do, tell you I was pregnant and trap you into staying?" She waved her hand around the air. "You would have resented me for asking you to give up your dreams and it would have killed any love you had for me."

He hated to admit it, but she had a point. He had been young and restless. And he might have felt trapped.

But he'd changed. Grown up. Seen what was out there and figured out what was important in his life. "I'm sorry I wasn't the man you wanted, that you needed back then."

Sadness tinged her eyes. "I'm sorry that I didn't tell you about Sam, but I honestly didn't want to hold you back. Then you would have hated me, Brett, and I couldn't have stood that."

"I could never hate you, Willow." He lifted her hand into his. Hers was trembling. Or maybe it was his.

"I'm sorry for so many things, for not being here for you, for leaving so that you let Leo into your life, and into Sam's."

"That's not your fault," Willow said. "That was my mistake."

Brett kissed the palm of her hand. "We both made mistakes, but Sam is not one of them. And

I'm not going back to the rodeo or starring in a movie."

Willow's eyes widened in surprise. "You're not?"

"No." Brett's heart swelled with love for her and his brothers and the land he'd once called home. He'd had to leave it to know how much it meant to him.

"I already told my agent, I'm done with rodeo, and that I don't want the movie deal."

"But Brett, it is a good opportunity for you."

"Maybe. But…I've wasted enough time. I want to be here."

"In Pistol Whip?"

He nodded. "I'm going to help Maddox run Horseshoe Creek." He grinned just thinking about his plans. "Being here will give me more time for you and Sam." He glanced at Sam, his heart nearly overflowing. "I promised him I'd teach him to ride."

Tears glittered on Willow's eyelashes. "He'll like that. That is, if that's what you want."

Brett took her other hand in his and drew her closer, then looked into her eyes. "What I want is *you*, Willow." He kissed her fingers one by one. "I love you and always have."

"But you're a wanderer, Brett. A dreamer."

"We can wander together," he said. "And I have lots of dreams." He pulled her to him and kissed her. "I've been dreaming all week about marrying you and the three of us living on the ranch. That cabin is pretty small and Maddox and Rose are in the big house, but I have enough money to build us a house of our own."

"But you gave up your money to get Sam back."

Brett shrugged. "That was just a small part of my savings. Besides, when Maddox made the arrests, he retrieved the stolen money. A portion of it will go to Eleanor, who has agreed to continue caring for Leo's grandmother."

"What about her husband?"

"I told Maddox not to bother pressing charges. The man wasn't bad, just desperate."

"That's generous of you, Brett."

He shrugged. "I guess I understand what desperation can do to a man. The rest of the cash will be divided among the ranchers the men stole from. He also recovered my hundred K."

Willow licked her lips. "I...don't know what to say, Brett."

"Say you love me, Willow," he said huskily. "That you'll be my wife."

Willow's mouth spread into the smile that he remembered as a young man; the adoring, loving one she'd reserved only for his eyes.

She looped her arms around his neck. "I love you, Brett. I never stopped." She stood on tiptoes and kissed him tenderly. "But you're giving me so much. What can I give you?"

"You've already given me the greatest gift of all. A son."

Willow toyed with the ends of his hair. "He is pretty special. I think he looks like his dad. He acts like him, too, sometimes."

Brett chuckled. "Then we're in for trouble."

Her look grew serious. "Are you sure, Brett? You won't get tired of being here? Of me?"

"I could never get tired of you, Willow. You're the only woman I've ever loved." He nuzzled her neck. "And there is one more thing you can give me."

Willow laughed softly. "What?"

He laughed and kissed her again. "A little girl."

Willow smiled and kissed him again, passion sparking between them just as tender and erotic as it always was when he touched her.

"Mommy, Brett, I gots cookies!" Sam raced toward him with cookie crumbs all over his mouth and they both laughed, then took his hand and walked along the creek.

Tonight they would tell Sam that Brett was his father, and that they were finally going to be a family.

And Sam would grow up a McCullen on Horseshoe Creek.

Brett could almost see his father smiling down at him from Heaven.

He would teach Sam to be a man just as his father had taught him.

Epilogue

Ray watched his brothers congratulate each other. Maddox married Rose. Brett was back with the woman of his dreams and had a son.

He wanted to pound their backs and wish them good luck. Tell them he was happy for them.

Find that kind of love for himself.

But the bitterness he'd felt for years ate him up inside like a poison.

Maddox and Brett still thought their old man hung the moon.

If they knew the truth, would they feel the same way? Or would they understand the reason he and his father had fought?

Maddox raised a glass of whiskey to make a toast, and Ray slipped into the shadows where he'd tried to stay all his life. He'd protected his brothers by keeping his father's secrets and lies.

As soon as the reading of the will was over, he'd leave Horseshoe Creek again. If he stuck around any longer, he might be tempted to tell them the truth.

But the old saying about the truth setting you free was a lie.

* * * * *

*Look for more books in USA TODAY
bestselling author Rita Herron's*
THE HEROES OF HORSESHOE CREEK
*miniseries in 2016.
You'll find them wherever
Harlequin Intrigue books and ebooks are sold!*

LARGER-PRINT
BOOKS!

HARLEQUIN

Presents®

**GET 2 FREE LARGER-PRINT
NOVELS PLUS 2 FREE GIFTS!**

PASSION
GUARANTEED
SEDUCTION

YES! Please send me 2 FREE LARGER-PRINT Harlequin Presents® novels and my 2 FREE gifts (gifts are worth about $10). After receiving them, if I don't wish to receive any more books, I can return the shipping statement marked "cancel." If I don't cancel, I will receive 6 brand-new novels every month and be billed just $5.30 per book in the U.S. or $5.74 per book in Canada. That's a saving of at least 12% off the cover price! It's quite a bargain! Shipping and handling is just 50¢ per book in the U.S. and 75¢ per book in Canada.* I understand that accepting the 2 free books and gifts places me under no obligation to buy anything. I can always return a shipment and cancel at any time. Even if I never buy another book, the two free books and gifts are mine to keep forever.

176/376 HDN GHVY

Name _____ (PLEASE PRINT)

Address _____ Apt. #

City _____ State/Prov. _____ Zip/Postal Code

Signature (if under 18, a parent or guardian must sign)

Mail to the **Reader Service:**
IN U.S.A.: P.O. Box 1867, Buffalo, NY 14240-1867
IN CANADA: P.O. Box 609, Fort Erie, Ontario L2A 5X3

**Are you a subscriber to Harlequin Presents® books
and want to receive the larger-print edition?
Call 1-800-873-8635 today or visit us at www.ReaderService.com.**

* Terms and prices subject to change without notice. Prices do not include applicable taxes. Sales tax applicable in N.Y. Canadian residents will be charged applicable taxes. Offer not valid in Quebec. This offer is limited to one order per household. Not valid for current subscribers to Harlequin Presents Larger-Print books. All orders subject to credit approval. Credit or debit balances in a customer's account(s) may be offset by any other outstanding balance owed by or to the customer. Please allow 4 to 6 weeks for delivery. Offer available while quantities last.

Your Privacy—The Reader Service is committed to protecting your privacy. Our Privacy Policy is available online at www.ReaderService.com or upon request from the Reader Service.

We make a portion of our mailing list available to reputable third parties that offer products we believe may interest you. If you prefer that we not exchange your name with third parties, or if you wish to clarify or modify your communication preferences, please visit us at www.ReaderService.com/consumerchoice or write to us at Reader Service Preference Service, P.O. Box 9062, Buffalo, NY 14240-9062. Include your complete name and address.

HPLP15

LARGER-PRINT BOOKS!
GET 2 FREE LARGER-PRINT NOVELS PLUS
2 FREE GIFTS!

HARLEQUIN®

Romance

From the Heart, For the Heart

YES! Please send me 2 FREE LARGER-PRINT Harlequin® Romance novels and my 2 FREE gifts (gifts are worth about $10). After receiving them, if I don't wish to receive any more books, I can return the shipping statement marked "cancel." If I don't cancel, I will receive 4 brand-new novels every month and be billed just $5.09 per book in the U.S. or $5.49 per book in Canada. That's a savings of at least 15% off the cover price! It's quite a bargain! Shipping and handling is just 50¢ per book in the U.S. and 75¢ per book in Canada.* I understand that accepting the 2 free books and gifts places me under no obligation to buy anything. I can always return a shipment and cancel at any time. Even if I never buy another book, the two free books and gifts are mine to keep forever.

119/319 HDN GHWC

Name _____ (PLEASE PRINT)

Address _____ Apt. #

City _____ State/Prov. _____ Zip/Postal Code

Signature (if under 18, a parent or guardian must sign)

Mail to the Reader Service:
IN U.S.A.: P.O. Box 1867, Buffalo, NY 14240-1867
IN CANADA: P.O. Box 609, Fort Erie, Ontario L2A 5X3

Want to try two free books from another line?
Call 1-800-873-8635 or visit www.ReaderService.com.

* Terms and prices subject to change without notice. Prices do not include applicable taxes. Sales tax applicable in N.Y. Canadian residents will be charged applicable taxes. Offer not valid in Quebec. This offer is limited to one order per household. Not valid for current subscribers to Harlequin Romance Larger-Print books. All orders subject to credit approval. Credit or debit balances in a customer's account(s) may be offset by any other outstanding balance owed by or to the customer. Please allow 4 to 6 weeks for delivery. Offer available while quantities last.

Your Privacy—The Reader Service is committed to protecting your privacy. Our Privacy Policy is available online at www.ReaderService.com or upon request from the Reader Service.

We make a portion of our mailing list available to reputable third parties that offer products we believe may interest you. If you prefer that we not exchange your name with third parties, or if you wish to clarify or modify your communication preferences, please visit us at www.ReaderService.com/consumerschoice or write to us at Reader Service Preference Service, P.O. Box 9062, Buffalo, NY 14240-9062. Include your complete name and address.

HRLP15